IN A COLD SWEAT

Also by roy glenn

Is It a Crime
Drug Related
MOB
Payback
Crime of Passion
Outlaw
Body of Evidence
Ulterior Motive
No More Tears in the End

Anthologies:
Girls from Da Hood
gigolos Get Lonely Too
Around the Way Girls 4

IN A COLD SWEAT

ROY GLENN

www.urbanbooks.net

Urban Books, LLC
1199 Straight Path
West Babylon, NY 11704

ISBN-13: 978-1-60162-268-6
ISBN-10: 1-60162-268-6

First Mass Market Printing April 2010
First Trade Paperback Printing April 2008
Printed in the United States of America

10 9 8 7 6 5 4 3 2 1

This is a work of fiction. Any references or similarities to actual events, real people, living, or dead, or to real locals are intended to give the novel a sense of reality. Any similarity in other names, characters, places, and incidents is entirely coincidental.

Distributed by Kensington Publishing Corp.
Submit Wholesale Orders to:
Kensington Publishing Corp.
C/O Penguin Group (USA) Inc.
Attention: Order Processing
405 Murray Hill Parkway
East Rutherford, NJ 07073-2316
Phone: 1-800-526-0275
Fax: 1-800-227-9604

Chapter 1

"Talk to me, Travis," Jackie screamed into her headset and hoped this time Travis would respond. It had been more than five minutes since she had lost contact with him. Just before that, Jackie heard what sounded like gunshots blaring in the background. She put on her night vision goggles, dimmed the lights on her stolen Hummer, and continued to search for him. "Come on, Travis, talk to me."

It was only now that Jackie began to realize why Nick Simmons's old partner, Monika Wynn, passed on this job and recommended that she and Travis do the same. After working with Travis on the surveillance of Martin Marshall, Monika thought that she could make use of Travis's computer skills. He had been a programmer by trade before the system dealt him a bad hand and he, in turn, became a high-tech robber.

Back in those days, Travis was known as Mr. Blue, Jackie was Mr. White, and their friend, Ronnie Grier, went by the name Mr. Green. They were all college graduates and all were victims of the corporate layoffs and downsizing. They'd rob banks, grocery stores, and jewelry stores. In this new career he had seemed to have mastered so well, his programmer's attention to detail proved useful in planning the jobs they ran.

That combination of skills was just what Monika, who was ex–army special operations, was looking for since she desperately needed a new partner. So when her contact, Jack Faulkner, approached her with this job, she brought Travis along to hear what he had to say. They met at Nita Nita on Wythe Avenune in Brooklyn. Over cocktails, Jack began to explain the job.

"Quad core processors," Jack said to Monika when she asked what the job was.

"What?" Monika asked, not having the slightest idea of the words Jack had just thrown at her.

"Quad core processors, Monika," Travis answered for Jack, seemingly excited at just the mention of the words. "It's a computer processor made for dual-processor servers, which means that these servers will essentially be eight-processor servers; two processors times four cores each."

"Oh," Monika simply said. "And this means something to me, why?"

"Multiplying the number of cores brings distinct advantages," Travis said, and Monika rolled her eyes. *He can be such a geek sometimes,* Monika thought. "First, it cuts down overall energy consumption for equivalent levels of performance."

"Aye!" Monika was less than enthusiastic. She turned to Jack. "You gotta excuse Travis."

"It's okay, babe. I like a man who knows the value of things," Jack said and raised his glass to Travis. At the same time he reached under the table for a briefcase and then handed a quad core processor to Monika.

She appeared unimpressed as she looked the small square object over carefully and handed it to Travis. "So, tell me again why I should be excited about this?"

Once Jack cut right to the chase and explained to Monika what they were worth and how much he'd pay them to steal a shipment of them, he had her undivided attention. But once he showed them a layout of the building and broke down the security, Monika said, "Thanks, but we'll pass."

A disappointed Jack stood up. "I understand. But think it over. If you change your mind, I'll be here same time tomorrow."

After they left Jack, Travis and Monika argued over why she turned the job down. "Too much risk, Travis," Monika said as she looked over to the passenger seat at Travis as she drove. "It's just that fuckin' simple. The level of sophistication on the security system Jack laid out is more than we need to be fuckin' with!" she shouted.

"Come on, Monika, I can handle it!" Travis shouted back, slightly offended at the chance that his comrade might be doubting his skills.

Monika took a deep breath and looked at Travis. "Then you do it." She returned her attention to the road.

Travis relaxed, and slowly a smile eased across his lips. "You serious?"

"Sure. If you're so fuckin' sure that you can handle

it, be my guest. Go see Jack tomorrow and tell him you'll do it. But if you do, don't look to me for any support. I'm talkin' equipment, personnel, intel, nothing," Monika said angrily as she accelerated, leaving smoke in her trail.

The next day Travis was back at Nita Nita to talk to Jack and accepted the job. The first person he came to was Jackie. She was the best getaway driver he knew. Naturally, she was down for anything that meant money. Since their other partner, Ronnie, had been murdered, Travis recruited Eddie Parker, a good man with weapons, to fill in his team. Parker's only assignment on this job was to watch Travis's back.

The processors were in a warehouse on Wales Avenue near Southern Boulevard by Bruckner Boulevard. Travis was confident that his skill at planning a job would minimize the risk.

But it didn't work out that way.

Jackie backed the Hummer up to the fence, and armed with AK-47's and nine-millimeters, Travis and Eddie Parker jumped over the fence on the far south end of the property. That was the only easy part of the job, as the perimeter was not secured with cameras.

Travis and Parker made their way toward the building under the cover of night. Once they reached the building they would have to disable the alarm system before they could go any further.

"You have to bypass an integrated security environment built around an access control system that is capable of capturing and processing any intrusion alarm system breach," Jack had explained to Travis when he accepted the job. "Door or window contact, glass breaking, or motion detection. It's sensitive to environmental changes like fire and temperature, so don't blow anything up. Even changes in the humidity in the joint will trigger an alarm," Jack laughed.

"How about we just shut down the power?" Travis asked.

"No can do. Change in video events, video motion detection, or even loss of video feed will set off the alarm. Now when that happens, pager alerts are sent to security with a video still in the form of a JPEG image; as long as the phone lines are attached to the access control server, of course. A prerecorded voice call is made directly to any phone, including mobile phones, which of course includes the police."

"How do we bypass it?" Parker asked.

Jack laughed. "That, of course, is your problem."

Now that they were at the building, Travis and Parker found as secluded a spot as they could find. Travis took off his backpack and pulled out a laptop computer to hack into the access control software. Days earlier he had done a test and was able to successfully access the system and navigate his way around without detection. In an effort to test security and police response time, Travis set off a fire alarm. Police and fire fighters were on the scene in eight minutes.

In addition to his laptop, Travis took out a c-guard cellular firewall, which he had used on jobs many times.

"What's that?" Parker asked.

"It is a cellular jamming device that broadcasts a junk signal. It floods the cellular frequencies, or sets up fake signals. Once I hack into their systems,

I'll engage the c-guard so the system loses its signal and cuts off communications between cellular handsets and its cellular base station, just in case we trip an alarm."

"But that's not gonna happen, right?" Parker made it sound more like a statement than a question.

"No. Because once I have access to the system, I'll be able to shut down all the security protocols and basically trick the system into thinkin' it's still active."

"You sure about that?"

"Trust me," Travis said and proceeded to his work. Once the system was in what Travis called safe mode, they entered the building and made their way—the objective without being detected. Travis opened the safe and then covered while Parker secured the processors in a backpack and put it on his back.

The trouble began right then.

Travis had just closed the safe, when the lights in the room suddenly came on. "Hold it right there!" the security guard yelled with his weapon drawn. Parker turned quickly and immediately opened fire.

"No!" Travis yelled. Parker had hit the security guard with two shots to the chest.

They turned off the light and walked out into the hallway where they were confronted by two more armed guards. Suddenly, lights came on and the wailing sound of the alarm rang throughout the halls. Travis fired a round of shots in the direction of security and he and Parker took off running in the opposite direction.

At the end of the hall, they were cut from the exit by more security, which opened up on them on sight. Travis and Parker ran down the hall until it forked off in two directions. Parker stopped and turned. "This way!" he yelled, shot wildly at security, and ran down the hallway.

"No!" Travis shouted to him. He had memorized the floor plan and knew if they went that way, they'd be trapped. "This way!"

Parker stopped in his tracks and ran back toward Travis, who was firing down the hall at security. "I'll cover while you make it across."

Parker nodded his head and Travis moved out into the open and fired. Parker ran out, but was hit almost immediately by a shot to his head. Travis watched Parker's body fall to the ground. "Shit!"

He was dead.

As blood oozed across the floor, Travis made an attempt to grab the pack from Parker's back. The gunfire was too intense and his body was too far away to reach without getting shot himself.

Upset that he was leaving without the processors, but thinking only about escaping with his life, Travis ran as fast as he could toward what he knew to be an exit.

Once outside the building, Travis made his way around the building looking for more security. He broke radio silence and called for Jackie. "Mr. Blue to Mr. White. Extraction necessary; proceed to the rendezvous poin—ahhh," he screamed in pain.

"Travis!" Jackie yelled, forgetting about their code names, but Travis didn't respond. He had been shot in the leg and couldn't make it back the way he came. Travis returned fire and as best he could, limped back inside the building.

As quickly as he could, Travis made his way to the front entrance of the building. He figured that with security looking for him outside, this would be the safest way to go. Travis felt himself getting weak. That's when he felt the pain and put his hand on the side of his stomach. He'd taken a bullet there as well and was losing blood.

Now at the front entrance, Travis stood in the shadows and peered out the door. He saw a security vehicle drive by and head toward the corner. Once the vehicle was out of sight, Travis opened the door and was startled by the alarm. He moved as quickly as he could down the street. Once he was far enough away from the building, Travis called Jackie. "Jackie!" Travis called out into his mike. "Can you hear me?"

"I hear you, Travis. Are you all right? I thought I heard shooting," Jackie said, relieved to finally hear his voice.

"I'm hit, Jackie," Travis managed to say. "One in the leg and the other in the gut."

"How bad is it?" Jackie asked excitedly.

"It's bad."

"Where are you?"

"I don't know exactly. I made it out of the warehouse, but I don't know where I am," Travis told her. He limped to the corner and looked up at the street sign. "I'm on the corner of One-hundred-forty-fourth and Wales by a transmission joint, hiding behind a blue Thunderbird."

"Hold on, Travis, I'm coming for you." It didn't take long for Jackie to find him. She got out of the Hummer to help Travis get in. "Where's Parker?"

"He took one to the head. He's dead."

"Damn," Jackie said, and got back into the Hummer. "I gotta get you to a hospital."

"No!" Travis shouted at her. "Call Freeze."

Chapter 2

Mylo sat in the corner of the room while the poker game went on; just as he did every night since Freeze put him in charge of the high-stakes game that Mike Black himself used to run. Black controlled a profitable and expanding business that now included real estate, entertainment, finance and construction companies, and burial services. But over the years, Black made his money in gambling, extortion, numbers running, and prostitution. Black and Bobby Ray started out collecting for André Harmon. Enforcing André's law earned Mike the nickname Vicious Black, but everybody called him Black.

Mylo had made himself useful—practically indispensable—to Freeze, but he earned the post after he snitched on Birdie and Albert. At that time, Freeze had convinced himself that they were responsible for the brutal murder of Mike Black's wife, Cassandra, but everybody called her Shy, except Black. He preferred to call her by her government name.

Mylo told Freeze that Birdie and Albert were hiding out in Atlantic City, and he and Nick took care of everything from there. Mylo was able to get that useful bit of information because he was not only working for Freeze, but selling drugs for Birdie and Albert as well.

It began one night when Mylo told Albert that he couldn't live off the scraps Freeze was throwin' him. Without telling Birdie, Albert gave Mylo a package, which he flipped and his buys got bigger and bigger until Mylo had become one of their best earners.

"And you're able to do this without Freeze knowing?" Albert had asked Mylo.

"They ain't organized like they used to be. Black and Bobby is out. They don't even fuck with the shit no more. I couldn't tell you the last time I even saw Bobby. I'm tellin' you, Freeze ain't the nigga y'all think he is," Mylo boasted.

Mylo knew that the time would come when he would have to get out, so before that happened, he wanted to have enough money to retire on. But there was another side of Mylo; one that Birdie and Albert, and certainly not Freeze, knew about. It was that Mylo was, in reality, a rogue DEA agent. His name was Clint Harris and he'd been working deep-cover assignments for the last five years. His job was to work his way into the target organization, gather information, and then bring the whole thing down. That had been his life, until his handler didn't show up for their weekly conversation. At that point, he was on his own. That was until fellow DEA agent Kenneth DeFrancisco brought him in. "You work for me now," DeFrancisco said when he first approached Mylo.

"What do I have to do?" Mylo asked.

"Exactly what you do. I put you in position, you make contact and work your way in, then report to me."

"No problem," Mylo responded, knowing that it couldn't be that simple.

"There's only one minor difference. You're not there looking for evidence of a drug conspiracy; you're there to create one."

It was DeFrancisco who put Mylo in touch with Albert; but then DeFrancisco went to jail and left Mylo out here again making crazy money with no handler.

Birdie and Albert's deaths were responsible for something other than Mylo getting a primo spot, running the game. It also gave birth to the Commission.

After Birdie and Albert's funeral, Mylo and several of the dealers that bought from them got together to pour out a little liquor for their homeys. It didn't take long before Black was the topic of conversation.

"You know it was Freeze that killed his boys," Bruce Stark told the gathering after his fourth drink. "In broad daylight at a red light," Stark testified.

"That nigga ain't no joke," Kevin Murdock, who liked to be called K Murder, confirmed.

Mylo laughed. "That nigga ain't all that, trust me."

"He bad enough to scare you out the game," Stark said quickly.

"True that. But I consider that health insurance."

"How you figure that, Mylo?" K Murder asked.

"These niggas claim to want to coexist peacefully with drug dealers, but the proof says that these muthafuckas delight in killin' drug dealers," Mylo said.

"You ain't told no lie there. Since Black made peace with Chilly, that nigga ain't done nothin' but kill muthafuckas," Steven "Cash Money" Blake said. "He killed Chilly and Rocky."

"I heard dude killed Chilly 'cause he was fuckin' Chilly wife," Billy Banner clarified.

"He still dead," Stark said.

"Sure you right," Cash Money agreed. "Then Black killed D-Train and now Birdie and Albert."

Mylo looked around the room. "Which one of y'all dumb niggas gonna be the next fool to try?" No one said a word. "What y'all muthafuckas need to do is get together."

"What you talkin' 'bout, Mylo?"

"I mean get together against Black," Mylo said and got up to leave. "Y'all stand a better chance that way."

A week later, Stark and Billy Banner, who everybody called BB, came to see Mylo at his apartment. At first Mylo was a little worried when he invited them in, but he figured if their visit was anything life threatening, Stark would have came with K Murder.

"Get y'all a drink?" Mylo offered.

"Whatever you got," Stark said and took a seat on the couch.

"Mind if I smoke?" BB asked and pulled out a blunt. He smoked blunts like they were cigarettes.

Mylo laughed. "Knock yourself out," he said before going to get the drinks. When he returned, Stark got to the reason for their visit.

"We decided to take your advice, Mylo," Stark began.

"Shit, y'all done fucked up now, if you doin' something I said." Mylo chuckled.

"Nah, it was good advice," Stark said. "I know you was drunk—"

"Shit, we all was," BB said and hit the blunt before passing it to Mylo.

"Before you left you said we stand a better chance coming up against Black if we worked together," Stark said.

"Organize," BB added. "Instead of competin' against each other, we work together; buy together. Get a better price. And if Black comes at us, we be together on that too."

"Now y'all talkin' sense. Damn, it was a good idea," Mylo said. "So who's in this little boys club?"

"Me, BB, Cash Money, and K Murder. We call ourselves the Commission," Stark announced.

"The Commission, huh?" Mylo asked and laughed a little.

"We wanted to know if you wanted in?" BB asked.

"No, thanks. I told you before, fuckin' with them niggas is bad for your health." Mylo paused and thought for a minute. "But you can consider me an adviser."

After they left, Mylo began thinking of ways he could use the Commission to his advantage. Right now, the only thing on his mind was making the most of this golden opportunity he had staring him in the face.

When Freeze put Mylo in charge of the high-stakes game, it surprised a lot of people, but Mylo had worked hard for it. Little by little, day by day, Mylo had done things to gain Freeze's confidence.

When the door opened and Freeze walked in at around one in the morning, Mylo sprang to his feet. "What up, Freeze?"

"Ain't nothin'," Freeze said and spoke with the players at the table before following Mylo into one of the bedrooms in the small house that he used for an office.

The time had finally come for Freeze. He now had complete control of the organization. Freeze had been running things for years, and naturally, he still got advice from Black. But now he was free to operate without any interference from anybody, including Wanda, who was the lawyer for the organization. Wanda was smart, careful, and just a bit ruthless. In addition to being their lawyer, Wanda managed the legitimate parts of their business and made a small fortune for her partners.

Now Freeze ran the show and he had come to the house to check on things as he did every night.

"What kind of night we havin', Mylo?"

"Been a good night. Philbert Cunningham done dropped damn near two hundred grand. We are definitely ahead tonight and it's early," Mylo reported.

"Good," Freeze said and looked at Mylo. "I may need you to ride with me tomorrow night."

"What up?"

"Collect some paper from Danny."

Mylo snapped his finger a few times. "Danny, Danny, Danny. I'm still tryin' to put names with faces. Big boy with the bad eye, runs books outta a sub shop on the avenue, right?"

"That's him. That nigga's skimmin'."

"You bullshittin'?" Mylo said and took a seat behind his desk. Freeze sat down in front of him. He sat looking at Freeze for a second. If Freeze thought Danny was skimmin', that meant he was going to die. And if he wanted Mylo to go with him, that meant he wanted him to kill him.

Mylo had been a DEA agent for six years, working deep cover for five of those. During that time he had never killed anyone. He had always assumed that this day would come and he'd always wondered if he could do it. Could he stand in front of a man, put two in his head and watch him die? Mylo wasn't sure he could, but he also knew what it would mean if he refused. Freeze would think he was a cop—which after all, he was—and kill him on the spot. That wasn't gonna happen.

"Just swing by and get me. I never liked that nigga anyway," Mylo said, and he didn't. "I'll get somebody to run the game," he offered.

"Don't you worry about that. I got that. You just be ready when I get here," Freeze said and stood up.

"What time?"

Freeze looked at Mylo like he was crazy for asking. "Just be ready when I get here, nigga, and stop askin' so many fuckin' questions," Freeze said and started to walk out of the office when he felt his cell phone vibrating in his pocket.

While Mylo left the office, Freeze glanced at the

display and saw it was his so-called woman, Tanya. She was lonely and hadn't seen Freeze in three days.

"What's up, baby?" Freeze answered.

"Just wondering when I'm gonna see you again," Tanya answered, getting right to her point. "I haven't seen you in days," she told him.

"I know that. I been busy."

"I understand that you have things to do, but you gotta sleep someplace, sometime, and it damn sure hasn't been here."

Freeze decided not to comment, and was glad that she didn't demand to know where he had been sleeping for the past few nights—and with who. If she had, he would have told her and she wouldn't have wanted to hear that truth.

Before he told Tanya, *Look, I'll see you when I see you and stop askin' me all them fuckin' questions,* he thought about Paulleen, the last woman he had neglected. "I'll be there in a couple of hours."

"I'll see you when you get here," Tanya said softly and ended the call. Tanya, like Paulleen before her, had grown tired of being left alone all the time. Assuming that Freeze was lying again, she briefly contemplated calling her new playmate, but then quickly discouraged herself after realizing that her playmate was working tonight. So Tanya just decided to wait and see if Freeze would actually show up.

When Freeze came out of the office, Mylo walked over to him. He handed Freeze a shot glass. "What's this?"

"Rémy."

Freeze drained the glass and handed it back to

Mylo. "That was smooth. What was that, Rémy Extra?"

"Louis XIII," Mylo said proudly. A few days ago, he ran up on a case of Rémy Martin Louis XIII. Mylo knew Black drank Rémy and thought it would be a good idea if he had some on hand if Black ever came there.

"How bettin' goin' for the fight?" Freeze asked, referring to the upcoming IBC middleweight championship fight.

"Heavy on the champ, just like you thought," Mylo told him. The champ, Frank Sparrow, was from the Bronx, and with his one-punch knockout power, was heavily favored to win. He was also a big-time poker player, a regular at the game, and had been since he started winning the big-money fights.

"Sparrow been here lately?" Freeze asked.

"Nah, ain't seen him since he started training."

"No shit."

"Yeah, they got him on lockdown. Got him up in the mountains or some shit."

"Mark my words, Frank Sparrow gonna find a way to bust outta that shit," Freeze said as his phone began vibrating again. "That nigga's weak for poker and pussy," he said and then pressed talk. "What's up, Jackie?"

"Travis has been shot," Jackie screamed as she drove away from the warehouse.

Chapter 3

Freeze turned away from Mylo. "I'll get with you later, Mylo," he said and started walking toward the door with his cell still in hand.

"Everything all right?" Mylo asked and followed Freeze to the door.

"Nothing for you to be concerned with." Freeze left the house and headed for his Navigator. "Okay, calm down, Jackie. Are you all right?" Freeze asked, wondering what they were doing for Travis to get shot.

"I'm okay," Jackie said excitedly as she drove down Southern Boulevard and merged onto Bruckner Boulevard. She looked in her rearview mirror at Travis. His eyes were closed and he was holding his right side with both hands.

"Where's he hit?"

"In the stomach and the leg," she said quickly. "He's losing a lot of blood."

"Where are you?"

"On the—um, on Bruckner Boulevard headed west," Jackie stuttered. Her heart was pounding and tears were steaming down her cheeks.

"Get on the Major Deegan and head uptown. But you gotta do something first."

"Okay—okay." She squeezed and twisted the steering wheel until her knuckles were pale, then sped up.

"Jackie, listen to me now. I need you to calm down."

Jackie tried to slow her breathing. She had driven them out of worst situations, but it was never like this. Parker was dead and Travis was dying in the backseat. Jackie looked back at Travis. "How you doin' back there? You all right, Tee?"

Travis moved and grimaced from the pain. "It burns, Jackie!"

"Jackie!" Freeze, who was still on the phone, shouted.

"What!" Jackie exclaimed.

"Stay with me, now. I need you to calm down. I need you to be cool and save his life."

"Okay, Freeze. I'm cool, I'm cool," Jackie said and tried to pull it together. "Just tell me what to do," she said nervously.

"I need you to do what you can to stop the bleeding," Freeze told her.

"What?" Jackie said. "I don't know how!"

"You can do this, Jackie. You don't want him to bleed to death before you get where you're going. You hear me, Jackie?"

"Yeah, yeah, okay. What should I do?"

"Find a secluded spot, get something to put over his wound and make him put pressure on it.

Then use his belt or something to wrap around his leg above the wound. I'll call you back and tell you where to go. Got me?"

"I can do this, I can do this," Jackie repeated as Freeze ended the call. She understood what she had to do to save her best friend's life.

Freeze got in his Navigator and dialed a number.

Tammy Crane began to stir in her bed when she thought she heard the phone ringing. This was her night off from Montefiore Medical Center and she had just drifted off to sleep.

Tammy worked as an emergency medical technician, assigned to an ambulance. She and her partner, Rico, let it be known to a certain clientele that for the right price they could use their medical services, no questions asked.

She opened her eyes and slowly realized that it was her cell ringing. Tammy rolled to the edge of the bed and reached into her purse. She looked at the display, saw the word *Freeze* on the screen and snatched it open. "Hello," she said in a whisper.

"Did I wake you, baby?" Freeze asked.

"Yeah, but it's cool. You coming over?" Tammy asked and sat up in bed.

"I was hopin' I was gonna catch you out in the street tonight."

"Why, what's up?" Tammy said and wrapped the sheet around her body.

"I need your help, baby, that's what's up," Freeze told her definitely.

Tammy could sense something was going on by Freeze's tone and that it wasn't her personal skills that he was in need of, but her professional ones.

"I got my stuff, so just come get me." In an attempt to lighten the mood she added, "I'll throw on some tight jeans, a T-shirt, and some pumps and I'll be waiting for you."

"You know how I love to see that fat ass in tight jeans and pumps. I'll be there in five minutes."

Meanwhile, Jackie thought about a secluded spot so she could try to stop the bleeding. Earlier in the day, she had dropped off a cold car in front of a abandoned building on 140th and Jackson Avenue, and she figured that somewhere around there would be the best place to go. When she found a spot with a dim streetlight, she turned off her headlights and parked the Hummer. Jackie turned on the interior light and hoped it wouldn't attract much attention as she climbed in the backseat.

"Travis, I gotta try to stop the bleeding," she said and Travis opened his eyes.

"What did Freeze say?" Travis wanted to know as Jackie began pulling up his shirt.

"Stop the bleeding and he'll call me back and tell me where to go. Come on Travis, help me pull this get up."

The two pulled up his shirt. "Ahh! That shit hurts!" he said, grimacing in pain.

When Jackie saw the bullet wound in his stomach and saw the blood coming from it, her body stiffened. She looked away and closed her eyes, but opened them quickly. "I can do this," she said out loud. *You have to do this*, she said to herself, and took off her leather jacket. After tossing it in the front seat, she began taking off her silk blouse. Jackie pulled at the material and tore it. She took the biggest piece and folded it a few time before placing it on the wound. "Hold that, Travis. Put pressure on it."

Jackie took the remaining pieces of her blouse and tied them together. "Lean up, Travis, so I can wrap this around you," Jackie instructed, doing what she had seen on television and in the movies hundreds of times.

Travis leaned forward and Jackie started to wrap her blouse around him. That was when she noticed that there was an even bigger wound on his back.

Jackie looked around the truck for something to put over that wound. She took a deep breath and unhooked her bra.

Travis smiled.

"What?" Jackie asked, and folded the cup.

"It's been a minute since I've seen the twins," Travis commented as Jackie placed her bra over the wound.

"Whatever, Travis," she said as she struggled to tie what was left of her blouse around him. "Sit back and keep pressure on that." With that done, Jackie turned her attention to his leg. She took off his belt and wrapped that around his leg.

Jackie climbed back in the front seat and turned off the interior light. She put her jacket on and started up the truck. "You okay?" Jackie asked as she drove away.

"Sad that the twins are gone," Travis managed.

"Yeah, you're all right." Jackie laughed and drove away. "What do you think I should do, go drivin' down the street with the twins hangin' out? Wouldn't be a good idea," Jackie said and got on the Expressway.

It wasn't too long after that when Freeze called. "Where you at," he asked once Tammy was in the Navigator with him.

"About to get on the Major Deegan," Jackie said.

"How's Travis?" Freeze asked.

"He's okay."

"Get off at One hundred seventy-ninth Street. You know where Roberto Clemente State Park is?"

"No," Jackie answered and frowned.

"Like I said, get off at One hundred and seventy-ninth Street and turn right on Sedgwick Avenue then make a sharp right at Cedar Avenue. Park by the bridge and wait for us there."

"On my way," Jackie said.

Once Freeze arrived at the park, Tammy wasted no time in redressing Travis's wounds. "You did a good job with this. Probably saved his life," Tammy told Jackie.

A short while after they arrived at the park, a silver four-door 2006 Acura RL pulled up and parked by the bridge. Jackie began to reach for her gun, but Freeze grabbed her arm. "He's with me," he told Jackie.

The man had come to pick up the Hummer that Jackie was driving. He would take the vehicle to a chop shop and Jackie could take Travis in the Acura. Once Travis was transferred to the Acura, Jackie took him home and put him to bed to rest.

"Jackie," Travis said. "Thanks for tonight."

"No problem." Jackie squeezed his hand a little tighter. "I thought I was going to lose you, man." Tears began to flow from her eyes.

"You saved my life tonight, Jackie. I'm never gonna forget that."

"You would have done the same thing for me."

"Yeah, I know." Travis looked away from Jackie and tried to decide how he was going to say what he had to say.

"What?"

"It's just that I coulda died out there, and for what? We didn't even get the processors, so it was all for nothing. Eddie died in there, died for nothing."

"What are you trying to say, Travis?"

"I'm out, Jackie. That was my last job."

"What?"

"I'm done. Finished with this shit."

"What are you talkin' 'bout, Travis. You can't quit now," Jackie told her wounded partner.

"Yes I can, Jackie. I don't need to do this anymore. I got enough money saved and my house in Connecticut is paid for. The economy is getting better, I could live good with a job and the money I got saved."

"Wow," was all Jackie could muster at the time. She let go of Travis's hand and sat back in the chair next to the bed. She wasn't liking the sound of this at all. *He can't be serious,* Jackie thought. *He can't just quit.* "Quitin', huh?"

"Yeah, Jackie, I'm done with all this. I mean, I got no real reason to keep doin' it. I just don't need to do this anymore."

Jackie stood up and bent over to kiss Travis on the forehead. "You get some rest. I'll be right outside if you need me." She had reached the door when Travis called out to her.

"Jackie."

"Yes, Travis."

"Thanks again."

"Get some rest and we'll talk in the morning."

Jackie went into the living room and plopped down on the couch. Out of reflex, she picked up the remote and started flipping channels. Not that she was watching or even cared what was on; her mind was on what Travis had just said.

In her mind, Jackie replayed the conversation over and over again. *I'm out. That was my last job. I got enough money saved and my house in Connecticut is paid for. The economy is getting better, I could live good with a job and the money I got saved.*

"Yeah, but what about me?" Jackie asked herself. Unlike Travis, who had a long-term plan for the money they had stolen over the years, Jackie spent all of her money on gambling, clothes, and her Porsche Cayman S that she dropped fifty-eight grand on.

Jackie rolled a blunt and poured herself a tall glass of Henny and thought about what she was going to do next.

Chapter 4

Mike Black

It had been a long time coming. With all that had gone on over the last year, I needed a night out. I hadn't been out in a while. Unless hangin' with Bobby counted, it had been some years. I'm talkin' about out with a woman. Have a good meal someplace nice, take in a show, do a little dancin' maybe, get some pussy; yeah, I was down for all that.

So I decided that we'd go to my favorite restaurant, McCormick & Schmick's on Fifty-second Street and the Avenue of the Americas. She ordered tilapia with roasted pepper and Cajun cream sauce. I had the swordfish with sun-dried tomato butter. The shit was off the chain.

After dinner we went to see *Les Misérables.* When it ran on Broadway the first time, it ran for sixteen years. Now it was back with a new cast, and we were both pretty hyped about seeing it. The story was about this guy in nineteenth-century France, who was always pursued by a righteous police inspector.

Sorta reminded me of Kirk and the way he's been trying to lock me up for years.

After the show, we hit the club and danced until the lights came on. I hadn't had a night like that in years, so I decided to tell her. "I really had a good time with you tonight," I said as we got to the car.

"Is that so? Well then, maybe we'll do this again real soon," she said as I opened the car door for her.

"You won't be able to keep me away from you," I said with my lips close to hers.

"We'll see," she said, without kissing me and got in the car. I shut the door and came around to the driver's side thinking that she was right. Tomorrow would come and I'd back to doin' what I do and not thinkin' 'bout dinner, the theater, and dancin'.

I started the car, but before I put the car in gear I turned to look at her. "You are so beautiful," I told her, because she was. I drove off thinking that she was the most beautiful woman I'd ever met, and I've met and had some beauties. "I can't wait to get you home, baby."

"I don't want to go there. Why can't you just stay *here* with me?"

"It's cool, baby, trust me."

"Michael, what's going to happen when we get there?"

"I'm gonna ease you out of that sexy black dress."

"That's not what I'm talkin' about and you know it. What's going to happen when we get there?"

I gripped the steering wheel tighter. "You let me worry about that."

"I don't wanna go."

"Why not?"

"You know what's gonna happen when we get there."

"Nothin's gonna happen when we get there."

"Not right away, but it's gonna happen." She put her hand on my face. I love it when she does that. "Bart is gonna be there, baby. And he is gonna kill me."

"No, he's not. I got him this time," I said and kissed her hand.

"That's what you said last time, Michael."

"I got a plan this time."

"You had a plan the last time and he still killed me. Let's not go home, baby. We could have so much fun if we—"

"I have to do this, baby," I told Cassandra as we pulled up in front of our house. The television was on in the living room and I could see what looked like Bart's silhouette standing off in the corner. I got out of the car and came around to let her out.

"Why can't you stay here with me? Why do you keep doing this, Michael? Why do you keep dragging us back here?"

I took my beautiful wife in my arms and kissed her; kissed her like it was the first time. "Can't you see? I gotta keep goin' in there until they're all dead."

I felt cold all over and I shook it off.

"Havin' the dream again?" Bobby asked.

"Yeah," I told him and ran my hands over my face. I looked over at Bobby. He was seated in his usual spot, in his recliner, in his basement. I had fallen asleep on the couch and was having the same dream I've been dreaming since Cassandra was murdered. I don't have the dream as often as I used to, but every time I do it changes. But Cassandra was right; he always kills her. It doesn't matter what I do, he always kills her.

This all began when I came back from Todos Santos, an island located at the Tropic of Cancer in the southern portion of the Baja peninsula off the coast of Mexico. I had gone there to kill Diego Estabon. A year before that, Diego had been the mastermind behind the kidnapping of my wife, Cassandra.

For that he had to die.

But when I got home I found Cassandra dead. Brutally murdered and the cops arrested me for her murder. I remember seeing her lying there on the floor and immediately dropping to my knees.

Both of her eyes were blackened, nearly purple; there were blotches of blood on her cheek. Her face was swollen so much I could hardly believe I was looking at my wife. My beautiful baby.

I remember there was so much blood, and there were bullet wounds in her back. Why would somebody do that to her? Every time I have that fuckin' dream I swear that I will find and kill everybody who I think was involved.

I really believe Kirk knows something. He's a good cop, and if it weren't for him, I'd probably still be in jail. Kirk may not know who hired the men who killed Cassandra—otherwise, they'd be in jail—but he knows something. I've tried talking to him about it; he said it was police business. Like I give a fuck about what's police business. Somebody knows who hired them, and I'll find them, and I'll kill them all. "How'd you know I was havin' the dream?" I asked Bobby.

"You always wake up in a cold sweat," Bobby replied. "Go ahead and say it."

"Say what?"

"About how you're gonna find the people responsible and kill them all." Bobby said the words to me that I always say.

"You doubtin' me?"

"No, I ain't doubtin' you."

"Then what are you sayin'?"

"That you always say that; that's all I'm sayin'. Shit! Why you gotta get all defensive and shit like a bitch?"

"So now I'm a bitch, huh?"

"You know what? Fuck you," Bobby said and got up. "Fuck you and this self-doubtin' bullshit. You lettin' that dream shit get to you."

"How so?"

"Okay, you say in the dreams you don't save Shy, never save her. As hard as you try, no matter what you do, Bart always kills Shy. Dream or not, what do you think all that 'I can't' shit rollin' around in your mind is doin' to you?"

At first, I looked at Bobby like he was a fuckin' fool. But then I thought about the dream I just had. *You had a plan the last time and he still killed me.* "In my dreams lately Cassandra's starting to doubt me. Maybe she represented the part of my subconscious that is starting to doubt myself." I looked at Bobby. He was looking at me like I was a fuckin' fool. "Did that make any sense?"

"A little."

"I could drive myself crazy tryin' to figure that out. All I know is that I will find the muthafucka behind it all, and I am gonna kill them."

Chapter 5

It was past midnight when Jackie left Travis's house. She got in her Porsche Cayman S and drove down Bronxwood Avenue on her way to meet Freeze. It had been almost a week since Travis announced that he was done.

"Damn," was all Jackie could say every time she thought about it. How could he just up and quit like that? Quit on her?

Jackie wasn't selfish. She understood that he had just got shot. "If the situation were different," she said out loud as she drove, "I'd probably be talkin' that same shit myself. But damn."

Jackie had allowed herself to believe that once Travis started feeling better he would change his mind, or at the very least, agree to do one last big job. At least that way she would have a stake to go forward with. But that wasn't the case. Travis was already up and around and had shown no signs of backing down.

At this point, Jackie knew that she was on her own and would have to come up with a plan if she was going to survive. She had briefly given some thought to trying to get a job as a chemist. After all, she had graduated from Rutgers University with a degree in chemistry and had worked for a few years at Frontier Pharmaceuticals before she was fired for insubordination after refusing to work on a project for Jake Rollins on her own time. But that was years ago, before she became part robber, part gambler.

"Maybe I'll put together my own robbin' crew?"

That was definitely a possibility, but she didn't have the planning skills that Travis had. She considered bringing somebody in to plan the job, but quickly abandoned that idea for one simple reason. "If they planned the job, what would they need me for?"

No, she would have to plan and control the job to run her own crew.

"If then else, Jackie. It's just the logical progression of events," Travis told her once when she asked how he came up with his plans. "If condition is true, the statements following then are executed. If condition is false, each *else-if,* if there are any, is evaluated in turn. When a true condition is found, the statements following the associated are then executed. If none of the *else-if* statements are true, or there are no *else-if* clauses, the statements following else are executed. Put simply, if this happens, then do this, if that ain't workin', what else can you do?"

"It can't be that simple," Jackie had questioned.

"The key is to anticipate every possible condition and plan for it."

"I can't do that."

"Yes, you can. I know you can. You play poker, right?"

"Yeah, but that's different," Jackie reasoned.

"It's no different. When you're playin' poker or any card game for that matter, you gotta always keep the objective in mind, naturally."

"Naturally?"

"You have to look at what you got to work with and anticipate based on that to determine what the other players have. That dictates how you're gonna bet or how you play your cards. Same shit I do when I'm plannin' a job."

"But when I'm playin', I'm doin' all that shit on the fly, in the moment."

"Okay, it's different, but it's the same. You just have to have discipline," Travis told her that day.

Jackie knew that was the one thing she had none of: no discipline whatsoever. A loyal slave to her passions was what Jackie was. If she saw it and she wanted it, she had to have it. And that included men . . . and women. And the Porsche she was driving.

Jackie was out on the island in Huntington driving down Jericho Turnpike when she saw the car on the lot. Jackie took in the Cayman with her eyes and immediately fell in love with its curves. The salesman told her, "The Cayman S is armed with three-point-four liters of total swept volume and a maximum of two-ninety-five horsepower at sixty-two-fifty rpm. Maximum torque is two hundred and fifty-one pounds-feet at forty-four hundred rpm."

"What's the top speed?" Jackie asked excitedly.

"One hundred and seventy-one miles per hour."

"I'll take it," Jackie stated, not even questioning the price tag on the vehicle. All she knew was that she wanted it, therefore having to have it; no matter what the price.

Lately she'd been thinking that the move might have been just a little impulsive, but she loved that car and the idea of selling it was out of the question.

Now, her plan was simple: talk to Freeze and convince him to let her into the poker game that Mylo ran. Jackie knew that Freeze was a creature of habit. She knew that Freeze would be at the house or on his way there. So when Jackie suggested that she could meet him there, Freeze was agreeable. She had to get in that game. She had fifty thousand dollars, which was fifty thousand less than it took to buy in. Jackie was hopeful that once she explained her situation that Freeze would still let her in the game.

When Jackie drove past the house she saw that Freeze's Navigator was parked a little ways down the street. She quickly parked her car and set the alarm. Once she told the doorman that she was there to see Freeze, she was allowed in the house.

Jackie entered the room where the game was being played and took it all in. She didn't see Freeze anywhere, but naturally all of the players turned to check her out, dressed as she was in tight blue leather. But quickly, they turned their attention back to their cards. Jackie's eyes were focused squarely on the pile of chips that sat in the middle of the table and wondered how much money that represented.

Mylo came out of the office and walked straight toward her. Jackie knew Mylo well enough to speak to him, but they had never really talked. She just never liked the way he looked at her like she was a pork chop sandwich. "What's up, Mylo?"

"You Jackie, right?" he asked, looking at her in exactly in the manner that she couldn't stand.

"Yeah." She knew if she planned to be in this game that Mylo was somebody she would have to deal with, so she would have to get used to it. "I'm here to meet Freeze. Is he here?" she asked even though she knew he was there.

"He's back here waitin' for you. Follow me." Mylo then said quietly, "With your fine ass," as he led Jackie into the bedroom that served as an office.

When Mylo opened the door, Freeze was sitting on the couch, talking on the phone. He looked up when he saw Jackie follow Mylo into the room. "I'll get with you later, Tanya," he said and pressed end on his cell phone.

Jackie smiled to herself when she heard Tanya's name mentioned. She knew her very well. One night, several months ago, Jackie was at Cynt's, one of the gambling houses that was run by Black's organization, when Freeze came in with Tanya on his arm. At the time, she was barely holding her own in the game when she looked up and saw Tanya looking at her. Jackie smiled back at Tanya. When Freeze went into another room to talk to Cynt, Jackie cashed out and went to talk to Tanya.

"Hi, I'm Jackie."

"Tanya. How you doing?" she said in a sweet and sexy voice that made Jackie want her even more.

Jackie took a step closer. "I'm doin' just fine tonight, honey."

"I saw you playing; how did you do?"

"Not too good tonight, but I held my own."

As the conversation continued, Jackie said, "I haven't seen you here before."

"Well, that's because Freeze doesn't like me to be around this stuff," Tanya said.

Jackie understood all too well why that was. Freeze's former girlfriend, Paulleen, used to be around all the time and used to be into everything and everybody. In fact, her former partner, Ronnie Grier, used to mess with her. Travis believed in his heart that it was Freeze who killed Ronnie. He remembered Freeze telling him one time when they were talking about how out of control Ronnie was and how that was bad for business. Freeze said, "Whatever I do is always business. Never personal, even if it seems that way. Remember that. And it will never have anything to do with you and me. Understand?"

Jackie wasn't as convinced as Travis was that Freeze killed Ronnie, but she had no intentions of asking. She looked at Tanya and understood why Freeze kept her on ice and far away from predators like herself. Tanya was a very attractive woman with a body that begged for attention.

Jackie recalled how her and Tanya agreed to go see *The One* at Impressions. They had a good time together and went out a few times before Jackie seduced her.

Jackie hadn't told Travis that she was sexing Tanya because she knew what he'd say. *Ronnie was fuckin' Paulleen and he died for it. What you wanna mess with another one of Freeze's women for? It's a death sentence.*

Now she stood before her lover's other lover about to ask him to do her a really big favor. "Jackie," Freeze said and got up from the couch to greet her. "What's up?"

"I'm good, Freeze, I'm good."

Freeze gave Mylo a look that told him that his presence was not needed. "I'll be out here if y'all need anything," he said, and after waiting briefly for a response from Freeze or Jackie—which didn't come—Mylo left the room and closed the door behind him.

"How's Travis?" Freeze said and sat down.

"He doin' a lot better. When I left to come here he was up and around."

"I'm glad to hear it. Now, what the fuck were you niggas doin' for Travis to get shot?"

"We were stealin' some computer processors and shit went south for us."

"How come I didn't know anything about this?"

Jackie was puzzled by the question. She knew that Freeze liked to be on top of everything that went on and insisted that Travis brief him before they did anything. But since he was asking the question, she knew that wasn't the case. "It was a job that Monika turned him on to. He'd been doing some jobs with her."

"I know that."

"Well," Jackie said and took a step back. "Monika

passed on the job because she thought it was too much of a risk, but Travis felt that he could do it, so we went for it."

"Maybe next time somebody tells you some shit like that, y'all should listen," Freeze told her definitely.

"That's not gonna be an issue anymore. After he got shot, Travis said he was done."

"No shit?" Freeze asked.

"Yup, that's what he said," Jackie replied and sat down next to him on the couch.

"I wouldn't worry too much about that, Jackie. Once he starts feeling better and starts missin' that paper, he'll be back."

"I thought that too, but he says he don't need to do this no more. That he got enough money saved and his house in Connecticut is paid for, and since the economy is gettin' better, he could live good with a job and the money he got saved."

"Yeah, well, we'll see," Freeze said and tapped Jackie on leg. "I'll talk to him."

"I don't think it will do any good, but by all means, get my boy back in the game."

"So where does that leave you?" Freeze asked.

"That's what I wanted to talk to you about."

"If I hear about somebody needing a good driver, I'll put you in."

"That's not exactly what I had in mind."

"So what's your plan then?"

"I was hopin' that you would let me buy into that game going on out there?"

"No," Freeze said flatly.

"Why?"

"'Cause I said so."

"Just like that?"

"Just like that," Freeze told her definitely.

"Why, Freeze? You know I'm good enough to play here."

Freeze looked at Jackie and paused. "You got the hundred grand to buy in?"

"Not exactly. I got fifty."

Freeze sat back on the couch and thought for a second. He liked Jackie and didn't really think she could afford to take all the money she had to risk on a game, but then he thought that her money was just as good as everybody else's. There was one other thing: Jackie had his back one night when he needed her. It was a debt that had to be paid. "I'll talk to Mylo and get you in the game. But the buy in is a hundred grand, which means you're fifty short. I'll front you the fifty for sixty back before you walk out of here, understood."

"Understood. And thank you," Jackie said as she left Freeze in the office. She knew that how she played that night would either make her or break her.

Chapter 6

Steven "Cash Money" Blake was starting to feel like the world was truly his. Since the formation of the Commission, he was able to buy product at a much lower price, so his profits were up, just like Stark said they would be. When they first came at him with the idea, he wasn't for it. Why would he want to get involved with that bunch?

Cash thought K Murder was crazy and that made him dangerous. They used to call him Nutso until he started killing people for it. In his opinion, BB was stupid, but he was the luckiest muthafucka he ever met. BB took over when his brother, Darryl, went to jail, a spot everybody knew he couldn't handle. But he had strong people around him; his brother's old crew who all knew that Darryl still ran things from his cell. It was only a matter of time before one of them would kill BB. His only real worry was Stark. Stark was just as ambitious as he was, but although Stark would disagree, Cash knew he was smarter.

Cash had his eye on the bigger prize. He wanted to be the king of New York; the next Nicky Barnes, who ruled the drug scene in the seventies. It was his destiny. And he saw this Commission as a way to make it happen. But he was patient. So when Stark announced that he would be the chairman of the Commission, Cash said, "I got no problem with that."

"You don't?" K Murder asked in surprise.

"Not at all," Cash assured, knowing that it wouldn't be long before K Murder would get tired of Stark's arrogant ass and kill him.

By that time the Commission would be organized and consolidated. He would be the one to see that it happened—in the interest of the Commission, of course.

"Then it's settled," Stark said with a confident smile on his face. "I call this meeting of the Commission to order."

Only Cash was smiling too.

Now Cash sat in the backseat of his Lexus on his way home with his new woman, CeCe, at his side. And he was still smiling as over the past few months he'd seen his plan was working just as he thought it would. There was already friction and mistrust between Stark and K Murder. Earlier that evening he ran into a few of BB's people and they told him that the crew was in disarray under BB's leadership.

As the Lexus turned down his street, it passed by a dark blue Ford 500.

"Team one to team two," the occupant of the Ford said into his headset.

"Go ahead," was team two's response.

"Subject vehicle has entered the box."

"Acknowledged, I have them. They're pulling up in front of the building now. Stand by."

"Acknowledged. Team one standing by."

Once Cash's lieutenant, Sly, put the car in park, two men came out of the building, walked down the steps and approached the car. The younger one went around and took the keys from Palmer, Cash's other lieutenant, while the other opened the back door for CeCe to get out. He extended his hand to her and she stepped out of the car.

CeCe winked at him and he whispered, "I'm'a tear that ass up when I get it."

CeCe giggled. "I'll call you in the morning," she said quietly as Cash came around from the other side of the car. She was a statuesque beauty who possessed the type of raw sexuality that made men fall at her feet, and Palmer was no exception. But CeCe knew that a lot would have to happen before she'd let Palmer see her naked thigh, much less get some pussy. But there was no harm in flirting.

"Take the car to the garage," Cash said.

"You got it," the kid said and hopped in the car.

After they went into the building, the doorman returned to his position in the foyer.

"Team two to team one."

"Go ahead with your traffic."

"Sentry's in the box."

"Acknowledged. Beta is moving into position."

"Acknowledged."

Two men got out of the Ford, which had been parked down the street. One immediately started walking toward the building. Once he had reached a certain point, the second man began walking behind him.

When the first man got closer to the building, his pace slowed and he began to stagger. Once he was in front of the building, he stopped, almost falling over in the process. He looked around for a second and then started stumbling up the steps. The sentry came out to meet him.

"Where the fuck do you think you're goin'?" the sentry asked.

"Inside," he said and dropped. When he dropped, the second man was in position at the bottom of the steps and hit the sentry with two shots. One to the head, the other in his chest.

"Sentry down, team two."

"On our way."

While team one dragged the sentry back in the building, the two men who made up team two joined them. One remained in the foyer to wait for the enthusiastic driver, while the other three went upstairs.

When Cash entered his apartment, he took his gun out of its holster and laid the gun on the dining room table as he passed it. He sat down in his chair and picked up the remote. As Sly sat down on the couch, Palmer went to pour some drinks.

CeCe walked over and kissed Cash on the cheek. "It's late, I'm gonna take a shower and go to bed," she said and kissed Cash again.

"I'm'a talk to the fellas for a minute and then I'll be right in," he told her.

"Don't be out here all night now," CeCe threatened.

"You don't have to worry, CeCe, we'll be gone before you know it," Palmer said as he poured.

"All right now," CeCe said as she turned her shapely ass around and headed down the hall.

"Good night, CeCe," Sly said as he watched CeCe swing her hips down the hall. He wanted to fuck her too.

Meanwhile, in the hallway, three men were putting on ski masks and moving into position outside the door.

Palmer came over and handed Cash a drink. "You know, if what BB's man said is true, we won't have to worry about him no more," he said as he sat down on the couch next to Sly and gave him a glass.

"You know it," Cash agreed. "But what I'm concerned 'bout is who gonna step up and take his spot."

"It don't matter who it is, you got them all in your pocket, Cash," Sly said.

"Sure you right, but I don't trust that nigga, Mays. He a snake and he on that rock. Ain't no tellin' where that nigga's head is," Cash told his lieutenants.

They were all startled when the door was kicked in and two men rushed in. As Sly dropped his drink and reached for his gun, the first shooter hit him with two to the chest. Palmer got to his gun, but the second shooter caught him in the chest before he could get a shot off.

Cash jumped up from his chair and tried to make it to his gun on the dining room table. Before he got very far, the third man entered the apartment and killed Cash.

He held up one hand, and each man went to his kill and put two more bullets to their heads. They quickly picked up their expended shells and left the apartment.

CeCe came down the hall after her shower, dressed in a white silk robe that hugged her symmetrical body. "What's all that noise out here?" CeCe asked as she came into the room. She screamed when she saw Cash's body laying dead on the floor. CeCe screamed again, ran back down the hall, locked the door, and called the police when she saw Sly and Palmer, with his gun in his hand, dead on the couch.

It was after dawn and Lieutenant Reyes, the head of the crime scene investigation unit, was just finishing up with Detective Sanchez of the narcotics division when Detectives Kirkland and Richards came into the apartment.

"Morning, Reyes," Kirk said.

"*Que pasa,* Kirk," Reyes replied and shook hands with Kirk and Richards.

Kirk turned to Sanchez. "Must be somebody special if it's got you up this early in the morning, Gene. What we got?"

"The one on the floor is Steven Blake aka Cash Money. He's a pretty big player in the game. Word on the street is that he had delusions of grandeur that he was gonna be the next big thing," Sanchez told them.

"Don't look like that's gonna happen for him," Richards quipped.

"Any witnesses?"

"We're canvassing the building, but so far, we got zip," Sanchez said.

"Who called it in?" Richards asked as Kirk knelt down next to Cash Money's body.

"Girlfriend. The officers said she was pretty hysterical and had to be taken to the hospital," Sanchez continued. "She told them that she was in the shower and this is how she found them when she came out."

"What's her name?" Kirk asked as he moved on to the couch where the other two bodies were.

Sanchez flipped though his notes. "Name is Cameisha Collins. Driver's license lists this as her address."

"Which hospital?" Richards asked.

"Montefiore Medical."

"What happened here, Reyes?" Kirk asked.

"Near as I can tell, the killers kicked in the door and caught them off guard. Looks like Cash Money there was trying to make it to his gun. That's it on the table over there. These two never got off a shot."

"No shit," Richards said and looked over the bodies on the couch.

"This one had his gun in his hand and the other was still in his waist," Reyes told them. "Very clean job, Kirk. All three took four shots. Two head shots, two in the chest, and from what I could see, the shooters didn't miss."

"They didn't?" Richards questioned and looked over the area where Palmer and Sly's bodies were.

"One more thing."

"What's that, Reyes?"

"I didn't find a single shell," Reyes told the detectives as his team prepared to leave the crime scene.

Sanchez took off his hat and ran his fingers through his hair. "You know what this reminds me of, Kirk?"

"What's that, Gene?" Kirk asked.

"You remember back in the good old days. We worked a crime scene just like this." Sanchez went and stood over Cash's body. "Nobody got off a shot; shooters didn't miss, one witness."

Kirk walked over and faced Sanchez. "Mike Black."

"See, that's what I like about you, Kirk; walking cop encyclopedia."

"So, is this like, classified, or can we all learn from the master?" Reyes asked.

"Vincent Martin," Kirk said.

"Never heard of him," Richards replied.

"Before your time, Pat. Maybe twelve years ago," Kirk told his partner.

"I keep telling you, Kirk, you could teach the kid some history. It'll make him a better cop," Sanchez said.

"You tryin' to say I ain't a good cop?" Richards asked and started walking toward Sanchez before Kirk stepped in front of him.

Sanchez held up his hands in surrender. "Easy, big man. I'm just sayin', history has a way of repeating itself."

"Just tell the story," Reyes said. "You know these old guys love to tell their stories." He patted Richards on the back a few times and that seemed to settle him down.

"It started after André was killed. André Harmon; you heard of him?" Sanchez began, but Richards interrupted him.

"Is this another Mike Black story?"

"You ain't know?" Reyes added.

"See, I did teach the kid something," Kirk said.

"So I won't bore you with the details of the war that went on after Black got out of the drug game. Anyway, before Chilly made peace with Black, the story goes that Black killed Jimmy Knowles and Charlie Rock. Vincent Martin went hard at Black until one night Black caught Martin and his whole crew slippin'. They were all at Martin's house chillin', just like these guys."

"Yeah, but there must have been eight, ten guys in there," Kirk added, pointing out the difference in the murder scene.

"Make a long story short, Black, Bobby, and Mr. Freeze busted in, killed everybody, except one guy."

"Why they leave a witness?" Reyes needed to know.

"To deliver a message to Chilly that he was next. After that, the war was over," Sanchez said and took a little bow.

"So you think Black did this?" Richards asked.

"I'm just sayin' there are some similarities, that's all."

"Yeah, but I don't think so, Gene. Black's been off the grid since his wife was murdered," Kirk said.

"Good story, though," Reyes said and left the scene.

"Come on, Pat, let's get some breakfast. Sanchez is buying," Kirk said and headed for the door.

"I am?" Sanchez said and followed him out.

"It'll give you a chance to tell some more stories," Richards said and watched as the bodies were bagged.

Chapter 7

"Wake up, Bobby!" Black said while shaking Bobby.

"Huh?" Bobby replied as he opened his eyes.

"Wake up. Let's get the fuck outta here, man."

Bobby began to stir in his chair. "Where you wanna go, Mike?"

"I don't give a fuck. I just need to get outta here."

"What about Michelle? Bobby asked about Mike's year-old daughter.

"I already talked to Pam. She's gonna watch her. Come on, man, get up and let's go."

Thirty minutes later, after Bobby finally got himself together, they were on their way to the Bronx. As they got closer to the city, Bobby again asked where Black wanted to go. "Let me use your phone," was Black's only reply.

"No. Why don't you get your own fuckin' phone?" Bobby asked.

"I don't like them."

"Oh, but you don't mind usin' them muthafuckas."

"I don't like being that accessible."

Bobby handed Black the phone. "Usin' up all my minutes."

"Damn, Bob, you want me to give you a fuckin' quarter?" Black said as he dialed. "Shit, you so fuckin' cheap."

"As a Jew prayin' at the Wailing Wall; but it ain't the money, it's the principle of the thing. You're always on mine when you could just get your own. That's all I'm sayin'."

"Whatever, Bobby." Black gave the ringing phone his full attention.

"What's up, Black?" Freeze asked when he answered the phone.

"Where you at?" was Black's reply.

"On my way to see how the game is going tonight."

"We'll meet you there." Black pressed end, dug in his pocket, and pulled out a dollar. He handed the phone and a dollar to Bobby. "Here, cheap ass. I don't have a quarter, but that should cover the call."

Bobby snatched the phone out of Black's hand but let the dollar drop between them. "I told you it ain't about the money," Bobby said as he drove.

"I know, I know, it's the principle."

Freeze pulled his Navigator in front of the house and put the car in park. He sat there for a minute thinking about the day that Black gave him control of the operation. It had been a few days after Shy's funeral before Freeze made it out to Bobby's house to see Black. He had meant to go the day after, but he got busy and the next day became the next day, but he finally made it.

The truth was, he wasn't in any hurry to face Black. He still felt responsible for Shy's death. "It's my fault she's dead," Freeze remembered telling Nick.

"Who, Shy? What the fuck are you talkin' about?" Nick had replied.

"Shy called me that night and asked me to come over there, but I never went."

"Why not?" Nick thought for a second. Then he looked at his friend. "You didn't go 'cause you don't like the way she talks to you?"

Freeze looked over at Nick, but didn't answer. Anytime they had business she would talk to him like a child.

"Before me and Black went to Mexico, I talked to Shy about that," Nick said.

"What you do that for?"

"Because you're my friend," Nick answered. "I told her how you felt about it. She had no idea. She called you over there to apologize to you."

Freeze didn't say a word after he heard that. What could he say? All Freeze knew now was that he couldn't carry that burden around any longer. He had to tell Black the truth. If he had been there, Shy would still be alive.

When he finally found Bobby's house, Bobby's wife, Pam, let him in and told him that Black and Bobby were in the basement and that he could go on down.

"There he is," Black said as Freeze walked down the steps.

"Missed the turn, didn't you?" Bobby asked.

"Every fuckin' time." Freeze went toward the bar. Once he poured himself a drink and refreshed everyone else's, he sat down on the couch next to Black. "How you doin'?" Freeze asked him.

"I guess I'm all right. I mean, I don't feel like killin' myself or no dumb shit like that."

"Yeah, but he been cryin' all damn day," Bobby added.

"Fuck you, Bobby. I ain't been cryin' all day," Black told him, although he did feel like crying at times that day. "Anyway, I'm glad you came. I want to talk to you about something," Black said to Freeze.

"What's that?" Freeze was curious to know.

"Me and Bobby been talking about this and I want you to run things," Black said, but Freeze didn't say anything. "I know you been handling shit for years, but it's always been somebody else, me, then Wanda, then Cassandra, callin' the shots. But that's over with. It's your time now. Me and Bobby are here to advise you if you need it, but you make the decisions."

"What about Wanda?" Freeze asked.

"What I tell you? You got this, without any interference from Wanda. I wish you had come yesterday while she was here so I could have told you in front of her. If you need her advice, ask her."

Freeze looked at Black, but didn't say anything. Feeling the way he was feeling, what could he say? Here he had just been handed everything he wanted and he felt empty.

"Bobby. I need to talk to Black for a minute." Freeze looked at Bobby, awaiting his response.

Bobby picked up his drink and stood up. "Holla

when you're done. I'll be at the top of the stairs listening," he said and winked.

Knowing how Bobby was, Freeze waited until he heard the door close before he said anything. "There's something I gotta tell you about the night Shy got killed."

"What's that?" Black asked and put down his drink.

"I was supposed to go over there that night," Freeze confessed.

"I know, she told me. Why didn't you go?"

Freeze didn't answer. He felt like a fuckin' fool having to say it.

"What ever it is, go ahead and say it," Black told him.

Once again Freeze found himself speechless. He finished his drink and took a deep breath. "I didn't go 'cause I didn't like the way she talked to me."

Black shook his head. "I know that was hard for you to tell me," Black said and got up to get the bottle. "You think it's your fault Cassandra's dead?"

"If I'd just gone over there, she'd still be alive," Freeze said while Black refilled his glass.

Black poured himself another drink and sat down. "You gotta let that go. It ain't your fault. They were listening on the phones; they knew you were coming and they went ahead with it anyway. What does that tell you? It means Bart was ready for you. So you drop that shit. You're gonna need a clear head for what you gotta do for me. You carryin' that guilt around ain't gonna do nothing for nobody; understand?"

Freeze told Black that he understood what he

was saying, and for the most part, he did. But there was still a part of him that still believed that if he had been there that night, things would have different, even if Bart was ready for him.

Before Black and Bobby got to the house, Freeze had spoken to Nick Simmons. When Freeze told him that Black was on his way there, Nick said that he had some information for Black and that Freeze shouldn't let Black leave before he got there.

Through his contacts, Nick was able to find out that the men that killed Shy were handled by a guy named Rosstein, but he died suddenly before he told who hired him. Now Nick had gotten information about Rosstein that might be useful.

"What's up, Freeze?" Nick said when he came into the office where Freeze and Mylo were.

"What's up," Freeze said and seemed to be looking around or past Nick. "You alone?" Freeze asked.

"Yeah, I'm alone," Nick replied.

"Where's Wanda?" Freeze asked and laughed.

"Fuck you, that's where Wanda is."

Freeze stood up like he was going to shake hands with Nick, but tapped him on the hip. "I'm just askin', 'cause usually she be right there attached to your hip."

Nick slapped Freeze's hand away. "Fuck you, Freeze."

Every time Freeze saw Nick without Wanda, he would kid him about it. She and Nick had sniffed around each other and denied that there was anything going on between them.

If you had asked Wanda, she'd say, "Nick?

Please, we are just two old friends that like to hang out."

While Nick had become notorious for saying, "Hangin' out with her is like old times, you know, when we all used to hang together."

That was until they finally got together one night while Black was in jail.

Since that night, they'd carried on a relatively secret relationship. That's the way Wanda wanted it; she didn't want anybody to find out, especially Mike Black. The only person who knew was Freeze, and although Nick was proud to have Wanda and wanted the world to know that she was all his, there were times like this that he wished Freeze had never figured it out.

"What's up, Nick?" Mylo said and got up. Freeze looked at Mylo and he started walking toward the door. "I'm gonna see how the game is goin'."

"Send somebody in with some drinks," Freeze ordered.

"Johnnie Black, right?" Mylo asked Nick.

Nick nodded his head.

When Mylo closed the door behind him, Nick looked at Freeze. "You got him well trained," he said and sat down on the couch.

"He serves a purpose. He hears shit; all kinds of shit." Freeze sat at the desk. "So where is the ball and chain tonight?"

"At the club waiting for me to come back."

"How long she give you to get back?" Freeze asked and Nick gave him a dirty look. "I'm just sayin', I'm surprised she didn't wanna come with you."

"I told her Black was gonna be here. She doesn't ever want Black seein' us together, much less knowing we're—" Nick started, but stopped and thought about what he would call their little arrangement. He didn't wanna just say they were fuckin', because it was more than that.

They did things together, but it was always in New Jersey or Connecticut. They couldn't take a trip together because Wanda was afraid of what people would think if they were both out of town at the same time. Nick didn't like hiding.

"Go ahead, say it," Freeze said.

"Say what?"

"Knowing y'all in love."

"Fuck you, Freeze," Nick said, even though it was the truth. He loved Wanda very much.

"Whatever, but y'all just think it's a secret. That nigga psychic. Black know all about that shit."

"He say something to you?"

"No. But think about that shit. Wanda be up in the club every night, actin' a goddamn fool every time a woman get near you and you don't think Tara ain't told Black?"

"Wanda ain't worried about Tara." Nick smiled as there was a knock at the door and Mylo returned with the drinks. Once he was gone, Nick said, "Tara caught us fuckin' above the stage one night."

"That used to be her and Black's spot. I know she couldn't wait to tell Black about that."

"Wanda knew that too, so she threatened her job. Wanda gave her a choice: Tara could tell Black and get fired, or keep her mouth shut and get a raise."

Freeze laughed. "Wanda gangster."

When Black and Bobby got to the gambling house, he went straight toward the office until he saw Jackie at the table. He stopped to watch her play out the hand while Bobby continued to the office.

When the hand was over Jackie pushed back from the table after racking in a hundred-thousand-dollar pot. She got up and walked over to where Black was standing. "Well hello, Mr. Black," Jackie said and stepped close to him. Black kissed her on the cheek and Jackie felt herself get a little wet.

"How you doin', Jackie? I didn't know you played here. I see it's goin' all right for you."

"It has," Jackie said nervously. She wanted to say something more, but couldn't think of anything clever.

"You done for the night?" Black asked.

"No, I just came to holla at you. I haven't seen you since—you know. I just wanted to—if you—we're all right?"

Black flashed a smile. "I'm okay, Jackie."

When Jackie saw him smile she wanted to offer herself to him on the spot. "I'm glad to hear that."

Black looked around the room and then back at Jackie. "I want you to do something for me."

"What's that?" Jackie asked, hoping that he wanted her to bend over and grab her ankles.

"I need to talk to Nick right now, but don't leave. We'll talk when I'm done," Black said and walked toward the office where Nick and Freeze were waiting.

It was after he dispensed with the pleasantries

and Mylo brought him a drink and left the room that Black turned his attention to Nick. "So what you got for me?"

"You remember the guy that told me how Shy was killed?"

"Yeah, Xavier Assante. What about him?"

"He told me that Rosstein had a girlfriend."

"So."

"It's a long shot, but she might know somethin'. Maybe not who hired him for that job, but she could tell us who he met with around that time."

"Where is she?"

"Hong Kong. X said he'd be there for a couple of weeks and will help you find her."

Mike sat down and thought for a minute. "What do you think, Bobby?"

"Worth a shot," Bobby said.

"Good, 'cause you're comin' with me," Black told him.

"I'll set it up," Nick said and got up to leave.

"Tell him we'll be there in a couple of days. I promised my mother that I'd bring Michelle down there for a while."

Freeze stood up. "Where you rushin' off to, Nick?"

"I need to get back to the club," Nick said and gave Freeze another one of those looks.

"We might come through there later," Black said to Nick as they all walked out of the office together. Freeze walked out with Nick, while Black stopped to wait for Jackie. She folded as soon as she noticed him waiting.

"What?" Bobby asked.

"I need to talk to Jackie," Black replied as she walked up to them.

"Hi, Bobby. How you doin'?" Jackie asked him, but it was obvious to Bobby that she was looking at Black.

"I need a drink, that's how I'm doin', Jackie. I'm'a go get us a drink."

"I'll be outside," Black said to Bobby.

"I'll be in the car waiting," Bobby said and walked off.

"Come on." Black took Jackie by the hand and led her out of the house. They walked down the street a little ways before Black stopped. "There's something I need you to do for me, Jackie."

"Just tell me what you want," Jackie said, eagerly.

"I want you to keep an eye on Mylo for me."

"You don't trust him, do you?"

"No."

"I don't trust him either," Jackie admitted.

"Why don't you trust him?"

"I just don't like the way he looks at me." Jackie laughed until she looked at Black and he was looking at her the same way. Only now it didn't bother her—in fact, it excited her. She knew she was hot for him, but she always thought that Black looked at her like a kid sister. Now to see that *I wanna fuck you* look in his eyes gave her hope that maybe one day her Mike Black fantasy would true.

"You keep an eye on him for me. I'm gonna be out of the country for a couple of days, but we'll talk when I get back. This is between you and me; no Freeze and no Travis, understand?"

"I understand," Jackie said excitedly, because

she knew it would give her a chance to use some of the surveillance techniques that she had learned while working with Nick and Monika.

"I heard Travis got shot. He all right?" Black asked.

"He doin' a lot better," Jackie said.

"Tell him I asked about him and give him this," Black said and handed Jackie the roll of bills he had in his pocket. "We'll talk soon."

Jackie watched Black until he got in the car with Bobby. She was overjoyed that Black thought enough of her to ask her to do something like that. This was better than sex, although sex with him would be good too. "Trust before sex. What a concept," Jackie said to herself as she walked back to the house.

Chapter 8

Mike Black

"Jackie's fine ass wanna fuck you," Bobby said to me as soon as I got in the car.

"What you talkin' about?" I asked him even though I knew.

"Don't play stupid. You know what I'm talkin' about. I can see it in her eyes; the way she looks at you. Jackie wants to give you some of that pussy, and you know it," Bobby said.

"I like Jackie."

"So—what's the problem?"

"I don't wanna like anybody right now." And I didn't. I don't know if I ever could or even if I wanted to feel for another woman what I felt for Cassandra.

"You a single man now. Get you a box of jimmies and fuck as many hoes as you can."

"Not worth the effort."

"What, fuckin' a bunch of hoes?"

"No. Fuckin' a bunch of hoes with condoms. It's not worth the effort."

"How you figure that? I really need to know why you think fuckin' ain't worth it. 'Cause I love fuckin'," Bobby damn near testified.

"I love fuckin' too. All I'm sayin' is that I don't like condoms. I don't know how you do that shit."

"You strap that muthafucka on and go for it. How the fuck you think."

"But I don't feel anything, Bob!" I said louder than I needed to, but I got my point across. But just in case I didn't, I continued. "I hate them damn things, 'cause I don't feel a damn thing. And they're tight."

"Get Magnums," Bobby said quickly.

"They're tight too." I could deal with the whole tight thing, but unless I feel it, it's like I'm just goin' through the motions, and after a while, I just lose interest.

That was another reason why I missed my baby so much. I loved fuckin' her. I couldn't get enough of her. There was never any need for anybody else. Everything I wanted, or could have ever imagined was right there.

I loved everything about Cassandra. The way she walked turned me the fuck on. Her eyes, her beautiful smile, the way she talked. Everything about her screamed, *Fuck me, Michael!*

"Whatever," Bobby said. "You'll get used to it."

"Whatever happened to the happily married man you used to be?" I asked more to keep him off me than anything else. Once Bobby gets on to something, there's no stoppin' him.

"Cat happened to him. That's what happened," Bobby said, talkin' about the woman he had an affair with. "Since her, let's call it, unfortunate incident, Pam hasn't felt like having sex."

"I didn't know. I thought, you know, once she got out of the hospital that, you know, it would—"

"I did too. But since it didn't go that way, I gotta do what I gotta do. Now, I give 'hem some money, bust a nut, and be back in time to pick the girls up from ballet."

I started laughing so hard I didn't notice that Bobby had started driving toward the Major Deegan like he was headed for the house. "Where you goin'?"

Bobby looked over at me and smiled. "Where you wanna go?"

"I hate people who answer questions with questions."

"Just answer the damn question," Bobby insisted.

"I was thinkin' we could ride by Cynt's," I told him, knowing he'd be down for it, knowing I'd have to listen to him talk shit about it on the way.

Bobby made a U-turn in the middle of 233rd Street. "I was hopin' you'd say that. All that talk about I don't like rubbers. Bullshit! I bet you used one on that amazon Shy look-alike?"

"You're right, Bobby, I did."

Her name was Maria Harrow and she dances at Cynt's where she goes by the name Mystique. She'd been dancing at Cynt's for years and I always marveled at how much she looked like Cassandra. I remember the first time I saw Mystique wasn't too long after I met Cassandra. I was at Cynt's with Bobby. We were at the bar talking to Sammy when something drew me like a magnet to the stage. I remember losing myself in the seductive manner that she moved her hips. The longer I stood there watching her, the more Mystique reminded me of Cassandra. I ended up giving her a hundred-dollar bill as a tip.

I ran into her about a month after Cassandra died. I had been in the city to talk to Wanda and was on my way back out to Bobby's house, when I stopped to get some gas. That's when I saw her. "Hey, Mike Black."

I was startled when I looked in the direction of the voice and saw what looked like my wife sitting in the car across from me. I thought my mind was playing tricks on me. At that time, I was having the dream all the time and it seemed so real. Like being awake without her was the nightmare that I just couldn't wake up from; because it was. But that day, I thought I had really snapped until she got out of the car.

Mystique was bigger than Cassandra. Taller. Five-eleven maybe, heavier, but there's not an ounce of fat on her. Her complexion, lips, facial structure, and her eyes; she had the same beautiful eyes. I wondered if Mystique and Cassandra could be sisters.

"Hey, how are you doin', Mystique," I said once I realized who she was, and more importantly, remembered what her name was.

We talked for a few minutes about the high price of gas and then about the run of nice weather we were having while she pumped her gas. "It has been nice for this time of year," I commented.

"Oh, I want you to know that I was sorry to hear about your wife."

"Thank you." I never know what else to say.

"I never met her, but everybody says she was a special lady," Mystique said.

"Thank you," I said again, 'cause I never know what else to say. "What about you? How you doin'?" I asked to change the subject.

"I'm okay. I'm startin' to get a little work during the day as a personal trainer. Still dancin' at Cynt's at night," Mystique said and I noticed the size of the thighs she had poured into those jeans. "Haven't seen you there in a while," she said and returned the pump to its cradle.

"I haven't been up there in years."

"You should stop by sometime and say hi to me," Mystique said and got in her car.

"I will," I promised and watched her drive off before I finished pumping my gas. Three nights later, me and Bobby were at Cynt's.

I lied and told myself that she wasn't the reason I all of a sudden wanted to go to Cynt's, but she was. Mystique smiled at me when she saw me walking through the room and I pretended not to notice. The whole time I was talking to Cynt and Bobby, I watched her when I knew she wasn't looking. I just wanted to watch her, watch her move, watch her talking, and I thought about my baby. Even though it felt good, after a while, I felt childish and stupid for doing it, so I finally walked over to her.

"I see you finally made it over here to see me," Mystique said and quickly dismissed the men that surrounded her.

"Yeah," I said over the music.

"Well, I'm glad you did." She quickly looped her arm in mine.

"I was gettin' ready to go, but I wanted to holla at you like I said I would before I left," I said in her ear.

She looked very disappointed. "Do you have to go?"

"Yeah, got some people I gotta see," I lied, knowing that I had nobody to see and started moving toward the door. Well, I had promised Pam we'd be back before Michelle woke up screaming bloody murder, which usually happened around one o'clock. I looked at my watch; it was almost midnight.

Mystique kissed me on the cheek. "What was that for?"

"That's to make you wanna come back when you got more time." She kissed me on the other cheek and then Mystique went back to work.

I intentionally stayed away from there for the next three weeks, thinking about what I was doing. Thinking about what I was thinking about doing. I wasn't in love with her or anything like that, but I was interested in her, and the only reason was because of who she reminded me of.

Was that wrong?

I didn't know, and I convinced myself that I didn't care. I mean, it wasn't like I was interested in developing a relationship with her. I just wanted to fuck her.

So I did.

Yes, I used a condom.

And then, she surprised me. When we were getting ready to leave the hotel, I offered her a thousand dollars and she turned me down. "I'm a dancer, Mr. Black, just a dancer. I'm not one of your hoes. I had sex with you 'cause I wanted to, 'cause I wanted you. Not because I knew you'd hit me off when you were done."

I was impressed, and not just with the fact that

she wouldn't take my money, but with Mystique. Maria Harrow definitely had skills and I wanted to fuck her again, so I did.

Yes, I used a rubber that time too.

Only this time I could tell how wet the pussy was even with the condom on.

And then she did it again.

This time I put the money in her hand, Mystique handed it back to me. She looked hurt that I even offered. I put my arm around her, you know, to console her. She kissed me; I kissed her, next thing you know I'm strapped up again and deep inside her.

After we were done that time, we're laying there and I said to her, "I like havin' sex with you."

She curled up next to me and I put my arm around her. "That's good, 'cause I like the way you do it to me. You've made me feel things that no man ever has. I could be givin' you money."

"Thank you," I said, 'cause I never know what else to say. "But there's one problem."

"What's that?"

I reached next to me and picked up a Magnum. "I hate these damn things. I wanna feel all this good pussy," I said and eased two fingers inside her.

Mystique smiled and rocked her hips on my fingers. "And this good pussy wants to feel all this dick," she said, smiling, and grabbed a handful of me. So the next day Mystique and I went to see my doctor and two weeks later we were having sex. Not plastic, but sex. Sweat poppin', pussy dippin' sex.

It was off the chain.

I had chosen wisely.

Only problem is, I'm startin' to like her.

And I don't want to like her.

When we got to Cynt's, I was able to walk up on Mystique at the bar without her noticing me. "Are you busy?" I whispered in her ear.

She turned around quickly and smiled. "Never too busy for you, Mr. Black," Mystique said and got up off of the stool. "Truth be told, I was hopin' you would come by tonight. I want to feel you inside me," she said and pressed her titties against me. Mystique was becoming very hard to resist.

She started out as an occasional convenience, somebody to release some tension with. Pretty soon we were getting together at least once a week. Last week, I fucked her three times and here I am again. "So can I steal you away from here?"

"I'll get changed," Mystique said quickly and walked away.

That's how we were together. We didn't talk much, a choice on my part, although Mystique does have a tendency to babble incoherently after she's cum a few times. But the more time we spend fuckin', the more time we spend talking. The more we talk, the more I realize that she's not just a Cassandra look-alike. Maria Harrow was just cool to be around. She's someone that seems to genuinely like me, but you never really know with women these days. It ain't like she don't know who I am and the kind of money I have. She could see the big picture and be positioning herself for the long haul. But from what I could tell, she's a nice person, one who I'm starting to like, and I don't want to like anybody.

Not now.

Chapter 9

Jackie arrived at the gambling house a little before eleven that night. It was to be her second night playing in the big game. The first night went relatively well for the most part. She hadn't come away the big winner yet, but she had left there each night with more money than she walked in with.

It wasn't always like that for Jackie. There was a time when she regularly lost money. That changed the night Mike Black told her about her game. "When you got money sittin' in front of you, you make reckless bets and when you lose, you try to laugh it off, like it's only money," he told her that night, after watching her lose a big pot.

"That's me," Jackie laughed, but she knew it was true.

"You chase the big pots. Greedy. And you chase them with weak hands and since we already talked about your inability to bluff, that makes you reckless and greedy."

"Damn," Jackie said slowly. "You really have been watching me."

"Watching you lose, Jackie. Watching you lose money to me." From that moment on, Jackie changed her approach to the game.

That night she was dressed in a red leather jumpsuit that hugged her curves, and made every man, and a few of the working women in attendance, stop to take notice. "You lookin' good tonight there, miss lady," Philbert Cunningham said. He was a divorce lawyer and a regular at the house. Cunningham considered himself a ladies' man and a reputation for seducing many of his female clients. He had been on Jackie since she sat down at the table that first night.

"Thank you, Mr. C," Jackie said and took a seat next to Earl, the dealer.

"You must think them tight-ass outfits gonna throw me off my game," Harold Ware said. He and his brother Stanley owned a construction company. They too were regulars, but Harold was there damn here every night, while his brother, who had a wife and children, only came once a week.

"You getting in now or you gonna wait 'til next hand," Sonny Edwards barked. Since he had been hemorrhaging money since he walked in, he wasn't in a good mood. Sonny was an older gentleman; he was retired but refused to say from what.

"I'm in, Sonny. What's the big blind?" Jackie asked as she organized her chips. The game was Texas hold 'em and before the game started, the two players posted blind bets. They were called *blinds* because they were made before the players saw any cards. The blinds ensured that there was some money in the pot to play for as the game started.

"Ten grand," Mr. C told Jackie. He posted the small blind of five thousand dollars, while Sonny put up the ten thousand as the big blind. Jackie put up ten grand to get in and the game began.

As the night wore on, Jackie found herself having a good night. She'd racked in a few big pots and was way ahead that evening. The *flop,* a term used for the three "community" cards that are dealt faceup on the table, were the ace of hearts, the eight of spades, and the six of spades. The fourth community—or *turn card*—was the ace of spades. Jackie was holding the ace of clubs and the six of hearts and she was feeling good about the two pair of aces she was looking at, and raised the bet by twenty thousand dollars.

Harold Ware played with his chips and stared across the table at Jackie, trying to get a feel for whether she was bluffing. Then he smiled and called her bet. At that point there was more than two hundred thousand dollars on the table.

The river, the final community card, was dealt. "Ace of spades," the dealer said.

"Twenty," Mr. C uttered.

Sonny flipped up his hole cards and took a peek. "I raise thirty."

"The bet is fifty to you, Jackie," the dealer said.

Full house, got 'em, Jackie thought and made her bet. "Seventy-five." She pushed her chips in and waited for the showdown.

"Well now, Jackie, I'm'a have to call you on that one," Harold said and pushed forward his chips.

"Showdown, folks," the dealer said.

Mr. C turned over his cards and pushed them toward the dealer and he arranged the cards with the community cards. "King and queen of spades. A flush," the dealer said and turned to Sonny.

He smiled a very satisfied smile and flipped over his cards. The dealer racked the two and eight of clubs. "Full house; eights full of aces. To you, Jackie."

Jackie looked at the four hundred thousand dollars in front of her and was sure that it was hers. Very slowly, Jackie pushed forward her cards. "Ace of clubs, six of hearts. A higher full house."

All eyes in the room were now on Harold Ware. He pushed his cards facedown to the dealer. "Five and seven of spades. A straight flush, four to the eight. Mr. Ware wins."

Jackie cursed and gathered together what was left of her chips. She backed away from the table and stood up.

"You ain't leavin', are you, sweetie," Harold said to her.

"Not as long as you got all that money sittin' in front of you. You don't have to worry. I'll be back in a minute to take some of it," Jackie assured him and headed for the bar.

The bartender had a shot of Hennessy waiting for her when she got there. Jackie didn't like drinking at the table. She thought it was too much of a distraction. It was more important to stay focused. While she sipped her drink, Jackie tried to figure the odds on Harold Ware having a straight flush. Lately, she'd been giving a lot of thought to what Travis said about planning. If then else. *Put simply, if this happens, then do this, if that ain't workin', what else can you do.* Could she really apply that same logic to poker? Could she plan a game?

No. Playing poker was more a matter of probabilities, the chance that something is likely to happen and drawing conclusions about the likelihood of those events. The theory was something she would work on at some other time.

Right now, she had a mission, and she had no intention of blowing it. Black told her to keep an eye on Mylo for him and that's what she was gonna do. During her little breaks from the game, Jackie had done her best, which wasn't very good, to plant listening devices around the house. Most didn't work at all, and those that did had a lot of static. When Jackie told Monika about it, she laughed and promised to come with her one night and clean up her work.

Jackie was about to return to the game when Frank Sparrow, the middleweight champion of the world, came through the door with two other men. The entire mood of the room changed at that moment.

In the short time that she'd been playing there, Jackie had heard all sorts of stories about Sparrow. He was a big-time poker player, who liked to throw around money and usually lost big money every time he came in the place. Everybody was glad to see Frank Sparrow.

Sparrow had grown up in Black's neighborhood and was loyal to Black for helping support his career. Jackie couldn't wait to get him at the table and decided to wait until he sat down to reclaim her seat at the table. In the meantime, she ordered another drink and sought out a spot to observe the champ and how Mylo, who had just come out of the office, interacted with the champ.

From her vantage point, Jackie watched Sparrow work the room. Talkin' loud, making round predictions on the fight, feinting punches on demand to display his hand speed and spreading around a little money to the few working women in attendance.

For his part, Mylo laid back and waited for Sparrow to make his way over there. Jackie looked him over carefully and could see that Mylo was a bit jittery and looked nervous as he watched Sparrow make it around the room.

Since her surveillance setup was suspect, when Sparrow finally got to Mylo, Jackie had already moved into position to overhear the conversation. "What's up, champ?" Mylo said and embraced him.

"I know you're surprised to see me, Mylo, but I escaped from lockdown for a few hours," Sparrow boasted. "They can't hold me. No man alive can stop me when I want something," he continued and feinted a few punches.

"Yeah, Freeze wanted to bet me that you'd make it here before the fight. Glad I didn't take any of that action."

"Is Freeze here?" Sparrow asked and pointed toward the office.

"He's not here, came through earlier."

"I wanted to holla at that nigga; see what y'all was talkin' 'bout," Sparrow said.

"You ain't gotta wait on Freeze, you can talk to me. I mean, that's how it's been all along, champ; you and me. Come here, let me put somethin' in ya ear."

Mylo led Sparrow into the office and Jackie cursed, because the device she place on the door frame had the worst static. Still, it was worth a shot, so she went into the bathroom to try and pick up the conversation, but there was way too much distortion for her to make out anything.

"Look, here's the deal. Bettin' been real strong on you to win, lot of action on what round you'll take him in," Mylo said as soon as he closed the door. "Everybody knows you're a slow starter. No one will think twice about you gettin' caught with a clean shot early."

It was almost a sure thing that Sparrow would win, but he often came out of the dressing room cold and had gone down in the first round three times. Sparrow was able to come back and win in each of those fights by knockout, but the consensus was that one day, Sparrow would get caught with a shot that he couldn't get up from.

"You go down in the first round," Mylo explained to the champ again. "Everybody says, yeah, it was bound to happen sooner or later. You said it yourself, they insisted on a rematch cause. You take the rematch and you kick his ass in the second fight. But you come away from here with a cool million, not to mention the guarantee money from the second fight, 'cause you know it's gonna be huge."

"I don't know, Mylo. Are you sure this is what Black wants me to do?"

"If he had known you were coming, he'd be

here to tell you himself. In fact, he was in here earlier tonight wantin' to know what you was gonna do. He said he was countin' on you to do this and was on me to make it happen."

Sparrow walked over and sat on the edge of the couch. He felt like he owed his career to Black for putting him onto a fight promoter who started getting him good fights. Still, it was a big decision, one he had thought long and hard about. He and Mylo had previously discussed throwing the fight and he ended up basically making up his mind that he was gonna do it, and that's the main reason he begged his trainer for a night out as long as he promised that there would be no gambling and no women.

"And this is what Black wants, right?" Sparrow still wanted to hear it one more time.

"He sat in that very spot and told me himself," Mylo assured Sparrow.

"Okay, tell him I'm in," Sparrow said and got up. "Tell Black I'm glad to do it for him."

"He'll be glad to hear that, champ," Mylo told him. *I know I am.* The truth was, Black and Freeze knew nothing about it. In fact, Mylo was still waiting for Black to actually speak to him. This was all Mylo's idea for Sparrow to throw the fight. Mylo would tell Sparrow that Black wasn't in on it after he had his money in his hand. At that point, what could he say?

Chapter 10

Mike Black

When Mystique was changed, we took a cab to our usual hotel. On the way, she told me about the drama that happened earlier at Cynt's. Two of the dancers got into a fight over a customer. "And she's holding the girl by her wave," Mystique said laughing. "And hittin' her in the face and sayin', 'I done told your skank ass 'bout fuckin' wit' my customers.' "

"She hurt her bad?"

"Busted her lips, her nose was bleedin' and her eye looked like it's gonna look fucked-up tomorrow."

"Little extreme, don't you think?"

"No," Mystique said definitely. "If any one of them bitches came anywhere near you, I'd kill their ass."

I laughed as the cab pulled up in front of the hotel, but she didn't. I looked in her eyes and knew she was serious.

When we got to our suite, as she always does, Mystique said she wanted to take a shower. She kissed me on the cheek and started for the bathroom. I unbuttoned my shirt and got a bottle of Courvoisier from the minibar. "Come here for a second. There's something I need to tell you," I said and sat down on the couch.

Mystique sat down next to me, took my face in her hands, and kissed me again. "What you wanna tell me, baby?"

"I'm gonna be gone for awhile. I'm takin' Michelle to the Bahamas to see my mother, then me and Bobby are goin' to Hong Kong."

Mystique looked devastated. "How long you gonna be gone?" she asked and curled in closer to me. I put my arm around her.

"I'll be back from the Bahamas in a few days, but I don't know when I'll be back from Hong Kong."

"Can I ask you what you're goin' to Hong Kong for?"

"I need to talk to somebody. Might take a while to find them." I didn't think it was a good idea to tell the woman I was about to have sex with that my only purpose in life was to find out why my wife was murdered. That nothing else mattered and that included her and how she felt about it, but that was the way it was.

"I understand." Mystique kissed me again. "I'm gonna go take a shower," she said and got up. I watched her walk away and thought about taking her with me. By the time the bathroom door closed I had decided against it. Takin' her to the Bahamas wasn't an option. Mystique was good people, and I liked her, but I had already decided that I wasn't gonna bring her or any other woman around Michelle, unless I was really serious about her. I wouldn't want Michelle to get used to somebody being in her life. Besides, Michelle doesn't really like women. Any time a woman holds her she cries. And I wasn't ready to bring her anywhere near my mother. I turned on the television while I drained the small bottle of Courvoisier.

Once I thought Mystique had enough time to be naked and in the shower, I got up, took off my clothes, and went in after her.

"Oh! You scared me," she said when I pulled back the shower curtain and stepped in with her.

"Who you think it was?" I asked and picked up the soap. She looked so good standing there, naked and wet with beads of water rolling down her beautiful dark skin.

"I didn't think it was you. Usually I find you laid out on the bed, rock hard, waitin' for me to wrap my lips around it," Mystique said and pressed her body against mine.

"You want me to go?"

"No!" she said loud and fast. "This just means you're gettin' more comfortable with me and that makes me happy." Mystique began planting kisses on my chest and then she looked into my eyes. "I know you only started seeing me because I look like your wife. And I'm cool with that. But I always hoped you'd see me."

"I do see you. And I like it." I ran my hands across her breasts and teased them with my tongue. I glided my tongue around her beautiful dark circles and sucked her nipples. Mystique took a step away from me and pressed her back against the shower wall. She raised one leg and spread her lips.

I like the fact that she's so tall 'cause it makes it easy for me to enter her while she's standing up. Once I was inside her, Mystique let her leg drop and pushed her legs together as tight as she could. She wrapped her arms around my neck and forced her tongue in my mouth.

There was real passion in her kiss. More than I had felt coming from her during any of our previous encounters. My surprise appearance in the shower and her interpretation of those events may have something to do with that. But I liked it, I like kissing, and it seemed like her mouth was designed to accept mine. I bent my knees a little deeper, pushed myself just that much deeper inside her, and tried to shallow her tongue.

I felt her thighs begin to quiver and Mystique pushed me off of her. "We gotta get outta here."

Mystique left me standing there in the shower and grabbed a towel on her way out of the bathroom. I laughed a little and turned off the shower. By the time I came out of the bathroom, she had dried herself off and was laying on the bed waiting for me.

Mystique rolled over on her back, lifted her legs and grabbed her ankles. "Come get this pussy."

I dropped my towel, walked over to the bed and then dropped to my knees. "Yeah," Mystique said, smiled and then nodded her head. "You know what this pussy needs."

Mystique spread her legs wider and I fingered her clit and felt her clit gettin' harder. She gently moved her body so I could taste her. I ran my tongue along her lips and licked her clit. Mystique moaned when I tasted her. I slid my tongue inside her and sucked her moist lips gently. I licked her with the tip of my tongue and her clit got harder. Mystique's body began to quiver. "Ooooh shit!"

When she couldn't take it anymore, Mystique pushed my head away. She quickly rolled to the other side of the bed and tried to catch her breath. I laid down on the bed next to her and ran my hand down her back and along that fat ass. I love touching her skin; it's so fuckin' soft.

Mystique rolled me gently on my back and got on top of me. I grabbed my dick and she eased herself down on it. She rested her head against my chest and started making circles around my nipples. Then Mystique quickly flicked her tongue at one. I liked that, so my body shook a little. She sat up and rode me slowly at first while I sucked on her nipples. When I started feeling her legs trembling on my thighs, I arched my back and pushed harder.

"That's it, baby. Fuck me," Mystique managed before she bit her lip and grinded her hips down on me. I pumped harder.

Then, all of a sudden, Mystique let out this gut-wrenching scream. "Aaaaaaaahhhhhhhh!" She rolled off me and tried to crawl away. But I wasn't havin' that. I quickly rolled off the bed, grabbed Mystique by her hips, and entered her slowly. Mystique began to moan and shake while I eased in every inch. She began winding her hips and I slid in and out of her effortlessly. Mystique was very wet, but she had excellent control of her muscles.

I let go of her hips and Mystique banged her ass against me. Mystique began to buck harder and harder. I squeezed her cheeks and did my damn level best to knock her back out. I leaned forward and grabbed Mystique by her shoulders. I began to pound that ass until her body started to tremble. "Ooooooooh shit, I like it like that!"

Yeah, I know.

I slowed my pace, pulling almost completely out of her, slowly easing myself back inside of her. I reached between her legs and fingered her clit with one hand and squeezed her breast with the other.

Then I thought I heard something in the other room. At first I thought it was the television, but when I heard it again I stopped moving. Mystique looked back at me like I had lost my mind. "Why you stop?"

I put one finger over my lips to quiet her. "Shhh." I eased myself out of Mystique and whispered, "Keep moaning."

I looked around the room for my guns. They were in the other room with my clothes. "Shit," I said softly and looked at Mystique. She covered herself but kept moaning like I asked her to. On the way to the door, I picked up the towel and wrapped it around me.

When I got to the door I put my ear to it, but I couldn't hear anything. Maybe I was just being paranoid, or had I really heard somebody out there? I looked at Mystique and she shrugged her shoulders. Just to be sure, I opened the door slowly and looked before taking a step. That's when I saw him.

I could see his reflection in the television moving into position to catch me coming out of the room. My guns were still sitting on the coffee table, but I'd be dead before I got to them. As soon as he got close enough to the door, I kicked the gun out of his hand and rushed him.

I caught him off guard and he fell to the floor. I punched him over and over again in the face. I grabbed him by his shirt and pulled him to his feet. I reached back and hit him again, only when I did, the towel fell off. So there I am, fightin' this muthafucka naked.

I reached to pick it up, and he caught me with a good shot to the face. When he swung again, I stepped to the side and wrapped the towel around his neck. He struggled to get that towel off his neck, but that wasn't happenin'. I pulled the end of the towel as hard as I could and rammed him face-first into the wall. That took some of the fight out of him. I jammed my knee in his back and pulled the ends of the towel until he slowly stopped moving. I kept the pressure on until his body went limp and fell to the floor.

I checked for a pulse to be sure he was dead and then went back in the room with Mystique. She was sitting on the bed with a gun in her hand. "Why didn't you tell me you had a gun?"

"You didn't ask," Mystique said and smiled at me.

After briefly considering getting back in bed with her like James Bond would have, I asked to borrow her phone. I called Freeze. "Who is this?" he asked.

"It's Black. I need a cleaner."

"Where you at?"

"I'm with Mystique," I said and pressed end. Mystique gave me a bewildered look. "Freeze always knows where I am."

"Okay, I can understand that, but what's a cleaner?"

"Somebody to get rid of the body and clean up the place so there's no trace he was here."

"The room's in your name, so I guess we can't just leave him here," Mystique said and got out of bed.

"Not an option," I said to her and watched her as she began to get dressed and considered picking up where I left off one more time. Yeah, Mystique was gettin' hard to resist.

Chapter 11

"I don't see or hear from you for days at a time. I have to practically beg you to come over here. When I do see you, it's only for a couple of hours and then you're gone again. We never go anywhere, we never do anything. You just come over here and fuck me once, maybe twice if I'm lucky, and then you're gone again and I never know when I'll see you again," Tanya told Freeze.

For his part, Freeze just sat there, listening to Tanya but not speaking. He had heard this all before, not only from Tanya, but from Paulleen. It wasn't that she was saying anything that wasn't true, he just didn't want to hear it.

Lately Tanya had been bringing the subject up more frequently, just as Paulleen had before her. Paulleen's solution to the issue was to fuck everybody. He wondered if Tanya would come to the same resolution. Freeze looked at her and knew the answer was yes, she would. He knew the easiest way to make your woman grudge fuck was to ignore her. But as long as Tanya showed him some respect and kept it out of his face, he really didn't care.

Maybe the whole havin' a woman thing ain't for you, kid, Freeze thought and stood up. "And we do go somewhere."

"Where?"

"The mall."

Tanya smiled. "Yeah, well, okay, there is that." The last time Freeze took Tanya shopping, he dropped damn near ten grand. Freeze may not have been around as much as she may have liked, but one thing he did know how to do was take care of his woman.

Tanya hadn't had to come out of her pocket for anything since her and Freeze got together. No mortgage, no bills, nothing. She had long ago traded her old Taurus sedan for a new Lexus LS 460. The note was taken care of monthly by the finance company that Black owned.

Over the past year, her real estate business had picked up and Tanya was able to bank all that money. And cash on hand was never a problem because Freeze always left whatever cash he had in his pocket on her vanity. "I can always get more cash," he would tell her.

Freeze started heading for the door. "Where are you goin'?" Tanya asked.

"I got someplace I need to be." *Anyplace but here,* Freeze thought.

"So that's your solution to the problem?" Tanya got out of bed and followed Freeze out of her bedroom. "That's your solution? You're gonna just leave?"

Freeze stopped and turned to face Tanya. She stopped suddenly when she saw the fury in his eyes.

"Yeah. This is my solution," Freeze said, walking toward her. Tanya started backing up. "I'm out. And when I'm gone, ain't no tellin' when you gonna see me again. Ain't that what you said?" By now, Tanya had backed her way back into the bedroom. "Ain't that what you said?" Freeze shouted.

"Yes," Tanya said softly.

"You think I wanna come out here to hear that shit? You know who the fuck I am. You know what the fuck I do. Now, all of a fuckin' sudden you got a fuckin' problem with it?"

"No, baby."

"I didn't think so."

"It's just that I love you, baby," Tanya said and meant it. She really was in love with Freeze; Tanya just wanted to feel some love coming from him. "I just wanna see more of you, that's all. Is that so wrong for me to wanna see and spend time with the man I love?"

"Whatever," Freeze said and started to leave again.

And once again, Tanya followed him out of her bedroom. She locked her arm around his as he continued to walk. Then Tanya got in front of him to block the door. "You not gonna give me some before you go, baby?" she whined with a sad face.

Freeze took out his gun and Tanya smiled. He took a deep breath and turned around. Freeze went back in the bedroom and Tanya gladly followed behind him. He put the gun under the pillow and took of his shirt.

Tanya allowed her gown to drop to the floor and stretched out on the bed. Once Freeze was undressed, he joined her. He lay on his back. "Go on, get you *some*," he said, imitating the way she said it and locked his fingers behind his head.

Tanya quickly took Freeze into her mouth and teased his head with her tongue. When he was rock hard, Tanya straddled Freeze and lowered herself into him. She slowly began to move her hips from side to side and slid up and down on him.

Tanya sat up and placed her hands on his legs, and then her feet on the bed and Freeze arched his back and thrust himself deep inside her. Tanya grabbed the back of his head and forced a nipple into his mouth. Freeze licked and sucked her nipple and Tanya's head drifted back. Her mouth opened wide and she screamed, "Shit!"

Tanya rolled off of Freeze, breathing hard, and positioned herself on the bed. She spread her legs as wide as she could get them. "Come on, baby—" That's when Tanya noticed that Freeze was out of bed and picking up his clothes. "Where are you going?"

"I told you I got someplace to be," Freeze said and headed for the bathroom.

"That's it?"

"You said you wanted *some*. You got you *some*. I got someplace to be," Freeze said and closed the door.

Now that he was out of Tanya's Mount Vernon

home and on his way back to the Bronx, Freeze took out his cell. "What's the word, Sergeant Adams? I know you got somethin' for me."

"Of course, baby. I always got a whole lot for you. You coming by here?" Tamia asked, hoping he'd say yes.

"I'll be there in about an hour," Freeze told her.

"I'll have it wet for you," Tamia said definitely. "Use your key," she added and ended the call. Even though she was a cop, Tamia was madly in love with Freeze and would do anything to make him happy.

Freeze knew how Tamia felt about him, but unlike with Tanya, who he had some feelings for, he discouraged it. "One of these muthafuckas in love is enough." Tamia was inside information on what the cops were doing. She was his very well-paid confidential informant.

As Tamia requested, an hour later Freeze was using his key to let himself into her place. When he stepped inside the apartment, it was in darkness. He started to call out to Tamia, but knew she wouldn't answer. Freeze took out his gun and went straight for the bedroom.

The room was lit with candles, one on each side of the bed. Tamia was laying facedown on the bed, wearing a pair of stilettos and nothing else. She had propped a pillow under her waist, so her ass was in the air. Freeze came around to the side of the bed and put his gun under the pillow. Tamia turned her head and looked at him. "Hi, baby," she cooed.

"What's the word, Sergeant Adams?" Freeze asked and began to get undressed. "Damn, you have a pretty ass," he said, sliding his hands across it and then along her lips.

"Thank you, baby. It's all for you," Tamia moaned and slid two fingers inside her. "It's wet and creamy, for you."

Freeze placed his hand on her wide hips. "You know that's how I like it," he said and spanked her cheek. Freeze got on his knees and entered Tamia slowly. While he glided himself in and out of her, Freeze smiled and thought about Tanya. Then he placed the weight of his body on his arms and Tamia rotated her hips; moving them slowly, then fast and then slowly again. Her body began to quiver as she stretched out her legs, trying to anticipate his movements.

When Freeze felt her tender lips touch his, Tamia tugged on his bottom lip and held it between hers. It didn't take long before she was kneeling down between his legs.

Freeze grabbed her breasts and squeezed them together before forcing both nipples into his mouth. Then he used his tongue to lick around her chocolate nipples. It was driving Tamia crazy and she instantly felt her juices flowing.

"This feels so good!" Tamia moaned, encouraging Freeze to keep doing what he was doing.

"You tasted so fuckin' good," Freeze pulled away from her swollen nipples long enough to say as she gazed into his eyes.

As Freeze bit at her nipples, he used his fingers to stroke and caress the wetness between her thighs. Before Tamia knew it, Freeze had eased her back onto the bed. He spread her legs a bit and parted her lips. He began using his tongue to flicker back and forth across her clit. Tamia could hardly concentrate, because Freeze was making it feel that damn good.

After that, Tamia rolled over and curled into the fetal position. She thought about how good her insides felt and her body began to tremble again at the thought of how hard she came and how many times. Tamia lay there holding herself tightly when she realized something. Something she hadn't expected.

Tamia rolled over slowly and Freeze was still lying there. Usually after finishing her off, he'd leave her shaking on the bed and be heading for the shower. She started to ask what he was doing, but she was afraid that he might move and she didn't want him to move. So she just looked at him, lying there with his eyes closed and his hands behind his head.

After a while, Tamia moved a little closer to Freeze and he opened his eyes. Tamia put her hand on his chest, waiting for him to move it and get out of bed as he had done many times before. When he didn't move it, Tamia cuddled up under his arm. She felt chill bumps all over her body when he put his arm around her.

"So what's the word, Sergeant Adams? I know you got somethin' for me."

"I see what you got for me," Tamia said and took him into her hand. "And I love every inch of it," she sighed and stroked him.

"Ain't nothing goin' on I need to know about?" Freeze asked. He wanted to know if she had heard anything that might make somebody want to kill Black. Things had been quiet lately, so he had no idea who would send somebody to kill Black.

When Freeze had arrived at Black and Mystique's hotel room, he had looked the dead man over. "Never seen this muthafucka before," he had told Black.

"Neither have I," Black confirmed. "I was hopin' you would know. You ain't doin' nothing I should know 'bout?"

"Not me. Just stackin' paper. I ain't been fuckin' wit' nobody. You ask her?" Freeze asked and pointed toward the bedroom where Mystique waited.

"Mystique? What you mean?"

"Jealous boyfriend?"

"I don't think so. I mean, I was lookin' at her when she saw the body. It didn't look like she recognized him."

"How we gonna get him outta here?" Freeze asked.

"I been thinkin' 'bout that. I say we pour a couple of bottles of gin down his throat and take him down the steps. If anybody sees us, we play it like he's drunk."

Black and Freeze were able to carry the body out of the room and down to the first floor without being seen. Once there, Mystique found a side door and they walked him out of the hotel. Freeze left Black and Mystique at the hotel while he took the body to the funeral parlor to be disposed of in the crematorium.

"Not a thing—well." Tamia paused and thought for a minute about the question Freeze had asked before continuing. "It doesn't have anything to do with you, but you ever heard of a dealer named Cash Money?"

"Yeah, I know that fool. What about him?"

"He's dead."

"Y'all know who killed him? Probably one of his boyz."

"Nope. They're dead too."

"How many was it?"

"Cash and four of his boys. The crime scene techs say it was a pretty clean shoting."

"What you mean?"

"All five took four shots. Two head shots, two in the chest. They said the killers didn't miss and Cash Money and them never got off a shot. No prints, no shells. Whoever killed them took the time to clean the scene."

"When did this happen?"

"Early yesterday mornin'," Tamia said and Freeze wondered why he hadn't heard about it.

Tamia laid her head on his chest. She figured now that Freeze had what little information that she had for him, that he would now get up and leave. But he didn't. Freeze laid there quietly holding her.

It didn't take long for Tamia to start getting excited. When Black was in jail, she had done Freeze a really big favor, for which she had only been partially paid. She got the cash she was promised, but to this point, he had reneged on the rest of the deal. Freeze had promised to stay the entire night with her. "You know, sleep next to me," she always said when she'd ask him about it. Tamia closed her eyes and silently hoped that this was the night.

Chapter 12

Mike Black

Jamaica was waitin' for me at the airport with five of his men when I got off the plane in Freeport. Like the good girl she is, Michelle slept peacefully in my arms through the entire flight. Sometimes I stare at her and marvel at the fact that I'm her father. That I am responsible for her existence. When I look at her I only hope that I'm worthy. I stepped out of the airport and felt the island sun beat down on me and immediately began thinkin' about putting all this shit behind me and just staying down there.

But somebody just tried to kill me and I had no idea why. Was it related to Cassandra's murder, or was this something else? I couldn't be sure of that one either. I had made a lot of enemies in my life; most of them are dead. It could be anybody wantin' to kill me over a whole lotta shit. I kissed Michelle on the forehead and hoped none of my shit would ever touch her.

tion about Mystique with my mother, his timing couldn't have been any better.

We spent the day going around to all the spots he ran on the island and stopped by one of the fishing boat operators, who took us out on the water for a while. I love the water. It's one of the things I miss most about not living in the Bahamas. When I get to New York, it's like I forget the water exists.

It was after sunset when the boat returned to Port Lucaya to dock, and I was ready to go home. But Jamaica had other ideas for my evening. "You must stay and take in the show tonight," Jamaica told me.

At the Port Lucaya marketplace there are stores, boutiques, and restaurants, outdoor and indoor bars, and cafés. On Friday night at Port Lucaya, they have a native Bahamian cultural show with fire dancing, limbo, and a stage show with the Port Lucaya dancers in the Count Basie Square.

I had seen the show many times before when I lived down there, so I wasn't all that hyped about seeing it again, but he insisted. "Besides, me want you to see the new girl that star in the show. Her really make a difference," Jamaica promised.

I was watching the limbo show and the great King Barry was working the crowd when I first caught a glimpse of her. "That her?" I asked Jamaica.

"Yah, mon, that her."

"What's her name?"

"Jacara Delbridge."

"She's very pretty." That was an understatement. She was beautiful. So beautiful that I couldn't take my eyes off her.

"Yah, mon, that her."

The show was great. Not only was Jacara fine as hell, but she could sing and dance her ass off. After the show was over, and the crowd of tourists had thinned, I was sipping overpriced Rémy at one of the outdoor bars when Jamaica came up behind me. "Mike Black," he said and I turned around. "This is Jacara Delbridge."

She was even more beautiful up close. I held out my hand and she accepted it. I felt her warmth. "Pronounce your name."

"Jacara Delbridge," she said slowly.

"It sounds better when you say it," I said, bowing slightly, and taking her hand to my lips. "I enjoyed your show."

"Thank you, I'm glad you enjoyed it," Jacara said.

The three of us stood there at the bar and made small talk for a while after that. Jacara told me that she used to be a showgirl in Vegas and concluded that she would never be the headliner so she decided to move on. She had come to the Bahamas for Junkanoo, a national festival in the Bahamas, on a short vacation eight months ago and decided to stay when the opportunity to be a part of the show presented itself.

Junkanoo groups "rush" from midnight until shortly after dawn, to the music of cowbells, in costumes made from cardboard covered in tiny shreds of colorful crepe paper, competing for cash prizes. Some say the word *Junkanoo* comes from John Canoe, the name of an African tribal chief who demanded the right to celebrate with his people even after being brought to the West Indies in slavery.

After a while, Jamaica faded into the background and disappeared. By that time, we were on our third round and the conversation had gotten comfortable.

"Can I ask you a question?" Jacara asked.

"Go ahead."

"Who are you?" she asked with a smile I was starting to like.

I turned and looked into her eyes. I liked those too. It's one of my weaknesses. Cassandra had the most expressive eyes. I used to tell her that they were like windows to her mind. "I'm Mike Black."

"I know your name," Jacara said and took a playful swing at me. "I wanna know who you are."

"What do you mean?" Jacara had me smiling.

"All night I've seen people who don't get in a hurry for anything, suddenly rushing around here. They're all nervous and intense. And then you appear, and they all but bow down to you," Jacara said and took a bow. "So again I ask, who are you?"

Now she had me laughing. "I'm Mike Black. I'm an old friend of Jamaica's."

"Hmm, that says a lot right there."

"I'm not even gonna ask what you mean by that."

"Of course not, if you did the conversation would continue and you might have to answer my questions. But it's okay. I don't like answering questions either."

"I'll remember not to ask any," I said and

drained my glass. "I enjoyed what conversation we did have." I held out my hand. "It was a pleasure meeting you, Jacara."

"The pleasure was all mine," Jacara said and politely shook my hand. "I enjoyed our conversation as well, Mr. Black. How much longer will you be on the island?"

"Another day, maybe two." I started walking and she looped her arm in mine.

"Maybe we can get together before you go. Say for lunch tomorrow?"

I stopped under a lamppost and looked at Jacara. "Where?" Something about the way she looked standing under that light moved me in ways that only Cassandra had.

"Do you know where the Paradise is?"

"I can find it." Especially since I own it. It's a club I own on the beach. The name is actually Black's Paradise, but nobody ever calls it that. I was planning on going there to check things out anyway.

"Meet me there at one."

"I'll be there. Good night, Jacara," I said and left her standing there. When three of Jamaica's men had to hurry to catch up with me, I heard her say, "Who are you, Mike Black?"

Chapter 13

It was after midnight and Wanda sat on the couch in Nick's office at Impressions, just as she had been just about every night since her and Nick got together. She had gotten up at seven-thirty that morning to make a meeting with a client at ten. It was the start of a very long day; especially since it was four-thirty when she and Nick got home from the club. By the time they finished doing what they did and had drifted off to sleep, it was after six.

Wanda cursed the alarm when it went off at seven-thirty, but she got up and did what she had to do. After a day where everything that could go wrong did, Wanda got home after seven. Her intention was to take a shower and get some sleep before Nick went to the club. But instead, she spent two hours on the phone with Pam talking about why Bobby had to go with Mike to Hong Kong. Wanda had just enough time to shower, get dressed, and be standing by the door when Nick was ready to go.

"You ready?" Wanda asked and let go of the yawn she was trying to suppress.

"Yeah," Nick said to her and picked up his keys from the table by the door. "I know you're tried, Wanda. Why don't you get some sleep?"

"I'm all right," Wanda said and opened the door to leave. Nick followed behind her, shaking his head. He knew there was no way to keep her from going. Nick would have never guessed that Wanda was so jealous and fiercely determined to protect her man at any cost. It surprised Wanda too.

There had been many a night when Wanda had stepped in between Nick and some woman who made the mistake of talking too long or standing too close to her man. After a while, Nick stopped going out on the floor while the club was open unless he had to. It was the best way to keep Wanda out of trouble. So every night the two of them sat in the office.

As the night wore on, Wanda's chin slowly touched her chest. She'd been nodding like that for the last half hour. Each time she'd open her eyes and glance over at Nick to see if he saw her and then go back to staring out the window at the dance floor below. This time when Wanda opened her eyes, Nick was looking at her. "Hi."

"Hi," Wanda said and fought off a yawn.

Nick picked up some papers on his desk and looked at them and waited for Wanda's neck to break again. She looked out at the light show, and before she knew it, her chin touched her chest again.

"Wanda," Nick said softly. "Wanda," he repeated. She slowly opened her eyes. "Why don't you let me take you home? You look like you need to get some rest."

"You sayin' I look bad?"

"No. I'm sayin' that you're sittin' over there sleepin'."

"I am not sleeping," Wanda insisted.

"Okay," Nick said and returned his attention to his paperwork. When Wanda nodded off again, Nick got up and knelt down in front of her.

When she began to open her eyes, Nick leaned forward. "Hi."

"Okay, so maybe I am a little tired, but I'll be all right. I don't have any appointments until after one tomorrow so I can sleep late. Lord knows I could use it."

Nick walked over to the bar and poured himself a drink. "You know you don't have to come up here every night."

"If I didn't, when would I see you?"

"Come on, Wanda, we see each other all the time. The club is not open every night and I see you when you get home before I leave." Nick smiled. "And you know I'll always wake you up when I get home."

"Yeah, right. You come home at five in the morning smelling like a bitch's perfume and that's my time?"

"Now we get to the real reason."

"What *real* reason is that?"

"You don't trust me."

"Yes, I do."

"No, you don't."

"Yes, I do."

"Whatever, Wanda. You don't trust me and we both know it. Everybody can see it but you."

"Did somebody say something?" Wanda asked, deathly afraid that Mike Black or anybody else had found out about her and Nick. Even though they were practically living together, she still didn't want him to know.

"Other than Tara, no."

Wanda rolled her eyes. "What did she have to say?"

"That's not important."

"Yes it is. It's important to me."

"What she said doesn't matter."

"Well, if she's got any comments, she needs to say it to my face. See what happens to her ass then."

Nick shook his head. "The point is that you don't trust me."

"It's not that I don't trust you," Wanda said and got up from the couch. She walked over to the window and pointed. "It's them half-naked bitches down there that I don't trust."

"Why? I don't want any of them," Nick said, joining Wanda at the window. "Wanda, I love you."

"I know that, Nick, but I just don't understand for the life of me why you have to chat up every half-naked tramp in the club."

"Other than the fact that it's part of my job, I can't think of any either."

"Oh, so now it's your job to flirt with every woman in the club?"

"I'm not even going there with you. You know damn well what my job is," Nick said and finished his drink.

"I just don't understand why you can't let Tara run the club. She does it anyway."

" 'Cause this is where Black and Bobby put me. So, what do you want me to do, ask them if they could give me something so that I could be off at night?"

"Yes."

"And what do I say when Black asks me why?"

"You could tell him that—" Wanda said quickly and then she paused.

"Those are the same ones I came up with."

"You could talk to Freeze."

"Freeze asked the same question."

"What's that?"

"What you want me to tell Black?"

Wanda rolled her eyes and walked over to Nick's desk. She leaned forward and put her hands on it. Nick stood back for a while and watched her bent over like that before he worked his way up behind her and lifted up her dress. "What are you doin' back there?" Wanda asked, smiling as Nick eased her panties down.

"Nothing."

Nick grabbed her hips and positioned her succulent ass exactly where he wanted it. He entered her slowly and Wanda began to squirm as he pushed himself inside her. She began winding her hips while Nick grabbed her shoulders and thrust his hips into her with so much intensity that Wanda had to steady herself. He plunged deep inside her before he exploded.

"I love you, Wanda," Nick whispered in her ear. "There's no one else for me."

Once they had fixed their clothes, Nick's cell phone rang. "What's up, Freeze?"

"I need you to ride with me. See if we can't find out who tried to kill Black."

"Where you at?"

"In the club."

"I'm in the office. Why didn't you just come up?"

"I didn't wanna interrupt nothin'."

"What you mean?"

"Tara say y'all be up in there fuckin' all night."

Nick looked at Wanda. "I'll be down in a minute," he said and ended the call.

"What does he want?" Wanda asked.

"He wants me to ride with him."

"Where?"

"See if we can find out who tried to kill Black."

"Somebody tried to kill Mike?" Wanda asked excitedly. "When did this happen?"

"The night before he left for the Bahamas with Michelle."

"What happened?"

"He was at a hotel and somebody broke in the room."

"And?"

"Black strangled him with a towel."

"The body?"

"The parlor," Nick said and armed himself.

"Why didn't you tell me this?"

"I thought you knew. I thought he would have told you since you saw him that morning before he left."

"No, he didn't say a thing," Wanda said, and once again felt left out. Black had always been overprotective of her through the years, but she thought that he would have at least mentioned that somebody tried to kill him.

"You want me to call you a cab?" Nick asked and picked up the phone on his desk.

Wanda started to ask why he couldn't take her home, but she kept it to herself. Instead, she sucked her teeth. "Go ahead."

As she rode home alone in the cab, Wanda thought about the way things were going. Black had always purposely kept her out of certain parts of their business. "Do the words *conspiracy to commit murder* mean anything to you, counselor?" Black would always tell her, but it was never like this. Now she felt isolated. She liked it better when she was the boss and Freeze had to answer to her.

When she got out of the cab, Wanda made her way to her door and fumbled for her keys as her cell began to ring. Sure that it was Nick, she dug the phone out of her purse. "Hi, baby."

But to her surprise, it was Glynnis Presley on the phone. She was an aide to a senator. Mike had been a heavy contributor to a few local congressional candidates over the years. Therefore, any time he needed something done, it was a simple matter to call Glynnis, and she would call the appropriate congressperson, who made the calls necessary for their problems to go away. "Wanda, it's Glynnis."

"What are you doing up at this hour?"

"I need to talk to Mike," Glynnis replied frantically.

"He's out of the country, Glynnis. What's wrong? Are you all right?"

"Yes, I'm fine, Wanda. I just need to talk to Mike, that's all."

"What about?"

"It's about his wife's murder."

Chapter 14

Mike Black

It was a little before noon when the car pulled up in front of Black's Paradise. I had arrived early for lunch with Jacara so I could check the place out. It felt a little weird being there. Cassandra and I had built that place and ran it together.

I hadn't been here since the day Cassandra was kidnapped and taken to New York by Diego Estabon's men. To me, it was the day that started this whole thing in motion. You see, I believe in cause and effect. The theory that for every action there is a reaction. If certain things happened, that would cause other shit to happen. The shit usually works to my advantage 'cause I'm usually the one pullin' the string. But there was another puppet master pullin' the strings.

When Cassandra was freed, she wanted to stay in New York instead of coming back to the island. "I feel isolated and trapped on this rock," Cassandra told me on more than one occasion. Cut off from the rest of the world, she'd say. So I decided to stay in the city. If I had listened to my better judgment and dragged her back to the Bahamas, maybe she'd still be alive.

I got out of the car and walked inside with my three bodyguards close behind. There were a lot of new faces working there; new bartenders, new waitresses, but Esmond, the cook, was still there. As soon as he saw me come through the door, he dropped whatever it was he had been chopping up and came out to greet me. I would have preferred that he drop the knife too, and so would my new bodyguards. "Whoa, mon," one said, and pointed his weapon. "Where ya tink you go with that knife?"

Esmond stopped in his tracks, put the knife down on the table closest to him and raised his hands.

"Its okay," I told him, and pushed the barrel of his gun down. "He's all right."

As soon as he felt it was safe to do so, Esmond rushed up and threw his big arms around me. "It's good to see you again, Black."

"It's good to see you too, my friend."

"The minute me hear you come, me fix conch chowder for you."

"I haven't had any conch since the last time you made some for me and Cassandra."

"I want to say how sorry I was to hear 'bout the lady," Esmond said, referring to Cassandra. "You know me love her like she me own flesh and blood."

"She loved you too."

"I miss her as I know you do," Esmond said and hugged me again. "You let me know when you ready for some conch." Esmond let me go and returned to his kitchen. "Maybe while you're here, we can get up a game. Since you been gone there no one to challenge me at chess."

"Why don't you bring me a big bowl and set up the board," I said and he smiled. Esmond loved to play chess and we had played many games and I had lost plenty of them because of careless mistakes. If I could just live my life without making careless mistakes.

Once I had gone through the place and met all the new employees, I settled down with a big bowl of conch chowder and wondered just exactly what I was doin' there. I mean, I did want to check out the place, but I wasn't pressed about it. To be honest, I was there for no other reason but to see Jacara, and I wondered why.

Okay, Jacara did have the type of body that made me want to play with it, so naturally I wanted to fuck her. But I had much more important things that I needed to be doing. The people responsible for Cassandra's death were still alive and thinkin' that they got away with it. And on top of that, somebody had tried to kill me and I had no clue what that's about.

The second that I finished my chowder, Esmond brought the chessboard over and began settin' it up. I hadn't played any since I left the island, so I was looking forward to playing even though I knew I'd lose. The game wore on and I tried to stay focused, but I couldn't shake the feeling that something just wasn't right. That something bad was about to happen.

I had just moved my queen's bishop to king rook two when Jacara walked in to the Paradise wearing a light blue sundress that hugged every delicious inch of her body. I watched her as she stood by the door and scanned the club looking for me. "Check," Esmond said.

I looked at the board, and sure as shit, he had me in check and had left me with few options. "Shit. Didn't see that," I said, realizing that I had made one of those careless mistakes.

By that time, the hostess had told Jacara where to find me and she was moving in my direction. When she saw me sitting there, her beautiful smile broadened. I stood up to greet her and so did Esmond.

"Well, hello, Mr. Black. How are you on this beautiful island day?"

"I'm good. Jacara Delbridge, this is Esmond," I said, pointing at the smiling chef.

"I must say that it is an honor to meet you, Miss Delbridge. I have seen your show and loved it, and have seen you in here many times." Esmond paused and pulled out a chair for Jacara to join us. "You might go as far to say that me a fan of both your voice and your beauty."

"Well, thank you very much," Jacara said graciously and sat down. "I don't mean to interrupt your game." She picked up a menu.

"That is all right, pretty lady. It is not going to last much longer," Esmond laughed while I studied the board trying to find a way to move out of check.

A waitress came to our table and placed a drink in front of me before turning her attention to Jacara. "Can I get you a cocktail from the bar?"

"Yes, I'll have a sea breeze with a twist of lime," Jacara answered.

What I needed now was to not only get myself out of check, but form a plan to turn this game around, mount some offense, and win this game. I had planned to be done with the game before Jacara got there. But now there she was, and I had no intention of losing in front of her. But I heard somewhere that roads are paved with good intentions and three moves later I heard Esmond say, "Checkmate."

Esmond stood up and collected the board and the pieces, while I sat there and wondered how I lost so badly again. "Can I fix you someting special? It would be an honor to prepare a meal for you," Esmond said to Jacara before he headed off.

Jacara picked up the menu again and began flipping through it, deciding what she wanted to eat. "Bahamian crawfish with peas 'n rice sounds tasty."

"I will make it with love, my dear," Esmond promised and turned toward the kitchen.

"You're not having anything, handsome?" she asked me.

I smiled. "He knows what I like. It's sort of a tradition we have. He puts it in front of me and I eat what he cooks."

"Isn't that sort of risky? I mean, suppose you don't like what he cooks?" Jacara asked and leaned forward, giving me a spectacular view of her cleavage. I couldn't tell if she was wearing a bra, but I hoped she wasn't.

"He has never let me down yet."

"I just don't know if I could do that," Jacara said, smiling, and touched my hand.

"Sure you can. Just think back to the days when

your mother cooked for you. You ate whatever she put in front of you, no questions asked."

"If you didn't, you'd get beat and then have to go to bed hungry," Jacara laughed and I enjoyed watching her titties bounce.

"Exactly."

"Still, I would really have to trust your cooking."

"He's a great cook. That's why I hired him."

"And that's another thing."

"What's that?"

"Why didn't you say that this was your place?"

"I thought you knew and that's why you wanted to meet here."

"No, I wanted to meet here because I like the atmosphere this place has and the food is good."

"So you didn't know this was my place and you didn't know the name of it."

"You know, as many time as I've been here, I never realized that the name of the place is Black's Paradise. Everybody on the rock just calls it The Paradise."

"Maybe I had you wrong, Jacara. Maybe you are just another pretty face."

"Since I am having a blonde moment, I'll take the pretty face thing as a compliment."

"It was meant to be one," I said to Jacara, thinking that she was as pretty as Cassandra and Mystique; if not prettier.

It wasn't too long after that when Esmond and a waitress came out of the kitchen carrying two plates. "Bahamian crawfish with peas 'n rice made with love for the beautiful lady," he said and placed the food in front of Jacara.

"Thank you, Esmond. It looks and smells

delicious. I know I'm going to enjoy it." Jacara turned to the waitress who had just put my food down and a drink in front of me. "Can you bring me another sea breeze, please?"

"No problem," she said and went about her duties.

"Excuse me, Esmond, but what is Mr. Black having?" Jacara asked.

"Me fix curried rock lobster with peas 'n rice for him, beautiful lady. Made with the same love as yours."

"That's not on the menu," Jacara protested. "If it was I would have ordered that."

"Me make it special for him," Esmond said.

"Ownership has its privileges," I said, and began eating my food.

"I tell you what, beautiful lady. I make you the same deal me have wit' him. When you come in, I fix someting special for you, just as me do Black."

"I'll have to let you know about that," Jacara told Esmond, who bowed graciously and disappeared back to his kitchen.

After we ate our food, I invited Jacara to join me upstairs on the observation desk. "I've never been up here before," Jacara said as we walked upstairs. "What's in there?" she asked, pointing to the door at the top of the steps.

"An office and a small apartment that my wife and I used to stay in sometimes when we didn't feel like goin' home." Which I hadn't gone in and don't think I'm gonna. Too many Cassandra memories in there.

"I didn't know you were married," Jacara said nervously like she expected Cassandra to bust though the door and bitch slap her.

"Don't look like that. She was murdered not too long ago."

"I didn't know. I'm sorry."

"How could you when you didn't ask." I started to say, "Don't be sorry for me. Be sorry for the muthafuckas that were behind it, 'cause I'm gonna kill all of them, just as soon as I find them." While it was the truth, why be a drag on the day.

When we got out on the deck and Jacara saw the view of the beach and the Caribbean Sea, it took her breath away. "This is an absolutely beautiful view from here. I didn't know this was up here." She moved to the rail and looked out in all directions. I was enjoying Jacara's company.

We spent the rest of the day out on that deck, just as Cassandra and I had done many times, talking and looking at the horizon until the sun disappeared from the sky. Since neither of us seemed to like answering questions, we agreed, no questions. She didn't ask me any more 'bout who I was or what I did, and I knew all I really wanted to know 'bout her.

When it was time for her to go, I walked her to her car. She took a step closer to me. "I enjoyed my day with you, Mr. Black, Mike Black," Jacara said in a way that reminded me a little too much of Cassandra.

"I enjoyed you," I said, 'cause I did. Mystique and I don't really talk much, so I enjoyed just talkin' to Jacara. But that's where things always get complicated. "Good night, Jacara." I gave her what amounted to a brotherly hug, you know, a pat on the back and an appropriate amount of space between us. But that wasn't enough for her.

Jacara wrapped her arms around me and I felt her lips against mine and I pulled her closer to me. I liked the way her body felt against mine, but I knew I would. With my eyes closed, I could see Jacara naked, sliding up and down on top of me.

"I like that," Jacara said.

I felt her body tremble a little in my arms. "Did you?" Jacara stepped away from me.

"Maybe we could continue this later?" Jacara stepped to my chest. "I'm at the Sheraton tonight. No big stage show or anything like last night at the Port. It'll be just me in the lounge singing old standards with a piano player. But stop by tonight, late," Jacara said and kissed me on the cheek this time. "If you're not busy, of course."

"Maybe I will."

"If you do, I'll sing 'Girl from Ipanema' a cappella for you. You did say that was one of your favorites?" Jacara said and got in her car. I watched her drive off before I told Jamaica's men that I was ready to go. And I mean, I was really ready to go.

As we drove, I thought about Mystique. I liked her, which is why I don't allow her to get close to me. It could be no different with Jacara. She was funny, intelligent, and very playful. She was fun to be with and I know I could get to like her too.

And would that really be all that bad?

Wanda tells me all the time that Cassandra wouldn't want me to be alone for the rest of my life. And for a second, I considered staying a while on the island. But I felt like I dishonored her memory being there on the island with Jacara. I was on a plane back to New York first thing that next morning.

Chapter 15

While Black dealt with his personal issues in the Bahamas, he was the topic of discussion at a meeting of the Commission in New York. Bruce Stark sat in the corner and looked out the window, while BB and K Murder argued back and forth about what they should do next.

"It was stupid to send one muthafucka to try and kill Black. Now Freeze got his whole set out in the street tryin' to find out who sent him. Where did you find that sorry muthafucka anyway?" BB asked.

"I brought him in from Cleveland." K Murder looked at BB without answering. He was tired of his shit and all that whining about this shit was getting on his nerves. "What your ass worried 'bout? They ain't gonna trace him back to you."

"And what if they do? What then?" BB demanded to know.

K Murder stood up and so did BB. "Then you'll just have to man up!"

"What you say to me, nigga?" BB put his hand on his gun.

"I said—"

"No, nigga, I heard what the fuck you said." BB took out his gun and so did K Murder.

The two stood silently with their guns pointed at each other, not saying a word.

"What?" Stark asked. "You two gonna shoot each other?"

Neither man answered.

"I didn't think so. Now put the guns down, sit down and let's get back to business," Stark commanded.

"Only business we got, Stark, is why you let this nigga be down?" K Murder asked.

"Muthafucka, don't you know I will kill you right now!"

"Make a move."

Stark got up and quickly snatched the gun from K Murder's hand and pressed it against his temple.

"What now, K? What else you got to say? I ain't BB. You fuckin' know that I will put a bullet in your brain and call my fat-ass Mexican maid to clean up the blood." Then he took out his gun and pointed it at BB. "And you, muthafucka? What you gonna do?"

BB lowered his weapon and sat down. "Nothin', Stark, we straight."

Stark handed K Murder back his gun. Once again, he pointed it at BB. "Bang," he said and sat down, but he kept his gun in his hand.

Stark looked at his two so-called partners and wondered how he ever thought it was a good idea to get involved with them. "You two make me fuckin' sick. Instead of us talkin' 'bout what we gonna do about Black, all you two wanna do is argue like little fuckin' bitches. K, I know Cash was your boy and shit, but BB is right. One fuckin' guy to kill Black? Come on, you should have known better."

"Yo, man, that's how your boy set it up. The plan was for him to catch Black in the pussy, walk in and cap 'hem both," K said in his defense.

"What went wrong?" Stark asked and got in his face. "Why is Black still alive and you ain't heard from your shooter?"

"I don't know what happened to him."

"I'll tell you what happened to him. Black happened to him, that's what happened. You should have sent two shooters and had a backup."

"Yeah," BB threw in.

K Murder looked at BB and decided right then that he was going to kill him. "Yeah, what?"

"You shoulda had at least two shooters," BB said.

"You come up with that on your own or you just repeatin' what Stark said?"

"Would both of you shut the fuck up!" Stark yelled.

"Fuck you, Stark. Black killed Cash and he's gotta die for that shit. I'm gonna kill that nigga myself. As for this nigga here and this fuckin' commission, I'm out. I'll handle my own business."

K Murder got up and backed out of the room with his gun drawn just in case BB wanted to get stupid. Once he was out of the room, he lowered his gun and told his boyz to come on.

During the ride down in the elevator, K Murder told his boyz what happened and that he had just quit the Commission. "It was a good idea, but it just had the wrong muthafuckas in charge, that's all. Fuckin' Stark thinks he's so fuckin' smart," K Murder said as they exited Stark's building and headed for their truck.

K Murder was too agitated by what had gone on with BB and Stark that he didn't notice the white panel truck that was parked across the street.

"Team one to team two," the voice said through the headset.

"Go ahead with your traffic," was the response from team two.

"Subjects have exited the building."

"Standing by."

Just before K Murder reached his Escalade, he stopped in his tracks. He turned to one of his boyz. "And that bitch-ass BB gotta die."

"Done," the man said and opened the back door of the Escalade for K Murder to get in.

"I want you to take care of that personally. None of that out-of-town shit, you hear me? And remind me to call Skyy in Cleveland and ask him what kinda muthafucka he sent me," K Murder said and got in.

As the Escalade pulled off, the panel truck fell in behind it. "Team one to team two."

"Go ahead."

"Subject vehicle is moving to your position. You should have them in sight right about now."

"I got them."

At that moment, a late model Impala pulled out into traffic just in front of the Escalade, with the panel truck right behind it. The three vehicles drove down the street and approached an intersection.

"Team two to team one. I'm in position."

"Proceed on my mark."

"Acknowledged team one."

"Three, two, one, mark."

The Impala slammed on his brakes and stopped.

"What the fuck?" K Murder yelled as his Escalade came screeching to a stop, barely avoiding rear-ending the Impala.

The panel truck pulled up alongside of the Escalade. The door opened and two men dressed in black with ski masks opened fire on the Escalade with Tec 9's.

People on the street ran for cover, while others dropped to the ground when the shooting began. The gunmen sprayed the Escalade with nine-millimeter shells. K Murder and his men never had a chance.

When Kirk and Richards arrived on the scene, a crowd of onlookers had formed. They were met by Detective Sanchez.

"What you got, Gene?" Kirk asked as he approached the bullet-riddled Escalade that the crime scene techs were collecting evidence from.

"The one in the back is Kevin Murdock, better known on the streets as K Murder," Sanchez informed the two homicide detectives.

"What's his deal?" Richards asked.

"Just another piece of shit dealer," Sanchez replied.

Kirk looked around the crowded street. "Anybody see anything?"

"Witnesses say that the Escalade had to stop short to avoid hitting the car in front of it. Then a white truck pulled up alongside. *Pop, pop, pop,* three body drop."

"What are you, a rapper now?" Richards asked.

"No, smart-ass, but here's something for you. This puke was a known associate of the late Steve 'Cash Money' Blake."

"The asshole that was murdered last week?" Richards asked.

"The same. Word on the street is that Blake, Murdock, and two others, Billy Banner and Bruce Stark—who, by the way, lives about three blocks from here—formed what they called the Commission."

Richards laughed. "These assholes kill me with this shit. The fucking commission. Give me a fucking break."

"Wait," Sanchez said. "There's something else."

"What's that?" Kirk asked.

"All four of them used to be Birdie's lieutenants," Sanchez informed them.

"No shit," Kirk said.

"It gets better. The Commission was formed not only as a buying co-op, but to protect themselves against your old friend, Mike Black."

"Now two of them are dead," Richards said.

"I have to give it to Black. Anytime one of these assholes gets too big they seem to die violently. Makes my job easy. It just creates work for you guys," Sanchez said and walked away.

"You think Black had them killed?"

"I don't know, Pat. Let's go ask him."

Chapter 16

Not knowing that a second commission member had been murdered, Nick and Freeze were in the streets as they had been for the last three days, looking for whoever tried to kill Black. During that time, they had talked to just about everybody they could think of that might know anything. "But nobody knows a fuckin' thing," Freeze said as he got back in his Navigator.

"Somebody gotta know something, Freeze. We just ain't found them yet," Nick said and Freeze took off. "I know I asked you this before, but you pissed off anybody lately?"

"I piss off muthafuckas every day, but if that was the case, then why would they go after Black? If somebody wanted to get at me, I ain't hard to find."

"Just askin'. So where you goin' now?" Nick asked.

"Black got a snitch named Manny," Freeze replied.

"I know Manny."

"Shit, everybody know Manny. He hangs out at some stops off the Concourse."

"You think he knows something?"

"Ain't no tellin', but we runnin' out of options and the last thing I want is for Black to get back tomorrow and we don't have shit to tell him," Freeze said as his cell phone rang. "What's up?" he answered.

"Freeze?"

"Yeah, who this?"

"Angelo Collette."

"Yo, What's up, Angelo?" Freeze asked. Mike and Angelo were in the same homeroom in high school. Back in the day when they both were freelancing, they did a few jobs together. Now Angelo was a made man with a crew of his own.

"I need to talk to Mike. He wouldn't happen to be with you, would he?"

"No, Black is out of the country. He supposed to be back tomorrow. Why?"

Angelo laughed a little. "Tell him it's nothin' major, but I need to talk to him when he gets back."

"No problem," Freeze said and was about to end the call.

"Ask him," Nick said.

"Hold on a second, Angelo," Freeze said and turned to Nick. "What you say?"

"Angelo hears a lotta shit. Ask him if he heard anything about Black."

"Yo, Angelo."

"I'm here."

"Somebody tried to kill Black a couple of days ago. You hear anything about that?"

"Black or white?"

"Huh?"

"Was the shooter black or white?"

"Black, why?"

"No. I didn't hear anything about that, Freeze, sorry. But I'm on it. I'll ask around, see if I hear anything. If I do, I'll let you know," Angelo promised.

"Good enough," Freeze said. "Why you ask if the shooter was black or white?"

" 'Cause it makes a difference."

"Yeah, I know. But why?"

"You just tell Mikey to call me," Angelo said and ended the call.

"What was all that about?" Nick asked.

"I don't know," Freeze said angrily. He didn't appreciate Angelo hangin' up on him like that. To him it was a sign that Angelo still didn't respect him.

Back in the day when Freeze was just getting started working for Black, people used to call him Black's little errand boy. Back then, one of Angelo's men used to talk big shit to Freeze. He remembered Black telling him, "Don't let him get to you, Freeze. Jimmy still fucks with you 'cause he knows it gets to you. Go ahead, you get out first. Make him show you respect. And remember who runs shit and who's always gonna be the errand boy."

Freeze got Jimmy's respect that day, and he knew that he would have to make Angelo respect him too.

After checking out a few spots, Freeze and Nick caught up with Manny Valdez. When Manny saw Freeze come in the bar, he took off running out the back door. When he made it into the alley, Nick was waiting there for him. "You in a hurry, Manny?" Nick asked and punched Manny in the face. Manny hit the ground hard.

"I don't know nuthin', I swear!"

"I haven't asked you any questions yet." Nick pulled Manny up off the ground and dragged him back to the car where Freeze was waiting.

"What's up, Manny?" Freeze asked as Nick pushed Manny into the car. "Where was you goin' in such a hurry?"

"I swear, Freeze, I don't know nuthin'," Manny said quickly.

Nick looked around and noticed that some people were coming out of the bar and coming toward them, and they didn't look happy. "Hey," Nick said to Freeze and pointed toward them.

Freeze nodded and opened the back door to his Navigator. "Get in," he said and pushed Manny inside. He tossed the keys to Nick. "Let's ride."

Once they were away from the bar, Freeze slapped Manny upside his head. "If you don't know nothin', why you run when you saw me?"

" 'Cause Black said he would kill me the next time he saw me."

Freeze slapped Manny again. "Do I look like Black to you?" he asked, and slapped Manny twice in the head.

"No!" Manny said and covered his head.

"I do see his point, Freeze," Nick said and laughed.

"Shut up, Nick."

"Black might have sent you to kill me. How could I know?" Manny continued to cover his head.

"That's all I was tryin' to say," Nick threw in.

"Somebody tried to kill Black; you know anything about that?"

"Is he dead?"

"I said *tried,* dumb ass," Freeze shouted and punched Manny in the stomach.

"He never was very smart." Nick shook his head.

"Shut up, Nick!" Freeze shouted, fighting back laughter. He turned his attention back to Manny. "What you know about that?"

"I swear," Manny said and made a cross over his heart. "This is the first I'm hearin' 'bout it."

"Stop the car, Nick," Freeze said and Nick complied. "If you hear anything, I better hear from you. Got that?"

"*Si, si,* I call you," Manny said.

"Good. Now get out," Freeze commanded.

"But my car is back there, Freeze." Manny pointed back toward the bar.

Freeze raised his hand like he was about to hit Manny again. Manny opened the door and got out running.

"What now?" Nick asked.

"Let's go by Incognito," Freeze answered.

"Incognito? You lookin' for somebody in particular?"

"Yeah. Little trick ho named Shonda works out of there sometimes. Maybe she knows somethin'."

"You got it."

Nick began moving in the direction of the club, but didn't notice that he was being followed by three men in a black Infinity.

When Nick and Freeze arrived at Incognito they went inside, ordered drinks, and looked around for Shonda, but she didn't seem to be there that night.

"I'm'a go take a leak. I'll be back," Freeze said.

"Hurry up."

"I know you in a hurry to get back to Wanda, but chill out," Freeze said and walked off.

As Freeze headed toward the bathroom, Nick looked as Freeze walked by the three men who had been following them in the Infinity. When he was passed them they fell in behind Freeze and followed him into the bathroom.

"What's wrong with that picture?" Nick put down his drink and fell in behind them.

Freeze went in the men's room and went into one of the stalls, just as the three men entered the bathroom. Nick was outside pushing his way through the crowd, trying to get to Freeze.

Once they were in the men's room, the three men drew their weapons and waited for Freeze to come out of the stall. Freeze flushed the toilet and was about to come out of the stall. He opened the door and saw three guns pointed at him. Before anybody could do anything, Nick burst through the door with both guns drawn.

Nick fired and shot two of the men several times

in the back of their heads. Freeze pulled his gun quickly and got the third man with two shots.

Freeze lowered his weapon and Nick stood over the bodies. "You recognize them?"

"Never seen 'hem before. You?"

Nick shook his head and put away his weapons. "Let's get outta here."

When Nick and Freeze came out of the bathroom, they made their way out of the club and back to the Navigator.

Nick tossed Freeze back his keys. "You sure you didn't piss anybody off?"

"I piss off muthafuckas every fuckin' day," Freeze said and drove away.

Chapter 17

Mike Black

When I arrived in baggage claim at JFK, the first person I saw was Bobby. It was when I noticed that Wanda was standing next to him that I got worried. If she was there, something was wrong, and whatever it was, it couldn't wait.

"What's up, Bob?" I said and shook his hand.

"How was the trip?" he asked.

"Good. Got to spend a lot of time with M. Jamaica took me around to all of his spots. Things are runnin' smooth down there. Good trip." I didn't even want to look in Wanda's direction, 'cause I really didn't want to hear what she had to say, but I knew I had to. "Hello, Wanda."

"I was wondering if you were going to acknowledge my presence," Wanda said and put her hands on her hips.

"That's because if you're here, something must be wrong and I'm in too good of a mood for you to drag it down." Even though I told her that it would be a while before she saw me again, I'd been thinkin' about goin' by and fuckin' Mystique before me and Bobby went to Hong Kong, and that was what had me in a good mood.

Funny how good pussy does that.

On the plane I thought about Jacara and how I ran off the island. That wasn't cool. I could have gone by the Sheraton and said good-bye to her. But fuck it, what's done is done. I wandered over to the carousel to wait for my bags.

"Oh, so I'm a drag now?" Wanda said and looked insulted.

Bobby and I looked at each other and started laughing. "Part of your job is to tell us shit we don't want to hear," Bobby said.

"It's what you do," I added and grabbed my bags.

Wanda's angry look slowly curled into a smile. "You two better be glad I love you," Wanda said and turned away.

Wanda started walking away from me and I looked at her hips swinging out the door. "You gaining weight, Wanda?"

"Why, do I look fat?" she asked as she looked herself up and down.

"Not fat," I said and tried to think of a delicate way to put it, but there wasn't one. "Just fat in the ass."

"Somebody must be hittin' that ass right," Bobby said and laughed.

Wanda spun around and looked at Bobby like he had just called her mama a two-dollar ho, rather than something she'd heard him say hundreds of times.

"What you talkin' 'bout, Bobby?" she said and got in his face.

"Nothing, Wanda. You know I'm just fuckin' with you. Everybody knows that you're the reincarnation of the Virgin Mary. Take some deep breaths," Bobby said and walked around her.

At first, I didn't think much of it, but as we got to the car, I wasn't so sure. Maybe somebody was hittin' that ass right and I had to think for a minute about how I felt about that. Wanda had been my other woman for a long time. Other woman that I wasn't fuckin', that is.

Me and Wanda had our time when we were kids, but we both agreed that we were better off as friends. Since then I've fucked more women than I could remember and I had been married, so why was I feeling jealous about somebody fuckin' Wanda?

Because she's always been my other woman, that's why! And I don't like sharing. I'll just kill the muthafucka, whoever he is, and that will put a stop to that madness. But that ass definitely was getting fat.

"So do you want to hear what I have to say or not, Mike?" Wanda said to bring me out of the fog I had just drifted in to.

"No, Wanda." Bobby opened the trunk and I put my bags in. "I already told you whatever you got to say can wait," I said and meant it. "Did you talk to Freeze about it?" I asked, knowing that Wanda really doesn't like taking her issues to Freeze. I think she misses carryin' power.

"No, Mike. I haven't talked to Freeze about it, because it's about Shy."

Okay, she had my attention. "What about her?"

"Oh, so now, because it's about Shy, you wanna hear what I gotta say?"

"Just tell me, Wanda," I said and got in the backseat.

"Move over," Wanda ordered and slid in the backseat next to me.

"Now I'm the fuckin' chauffeur?" Bobby complained.

"Just drive, Bobby. You know this is important," Wanda said in her stern voice, and that shut Bobby up for the moment.

"What about Cassandra?"

"I got a call late last night from Glynnis."

"Presley?"

"Yes. She said that it was important that she talk to you."

"She say what it was about?"

"Only that it was about Shy. Whatever it's about, Glynnis sounded scared, Mike."

"Get her on the phone," I said and wondered what Glynnis could possibly know about Cassandra. I can't even say for sure that Glynnis ever met her.

I watched as Wanda dug around in her big-ass purse for her cell. "Here," Bobby said. "Use mine." He tried to hand the phone to Wanda.

"Now what makes you think I know her number? I don't know anybody's number anymore."

Once Wanda found her phone and got past Glynnis's personal assistant, which I thought was odd for a Sunday morning, Glynnis finally came to the phone. "It's Wanda, Glynnis. I have Mike with me. He wants to talk to you."

Whatever Glynnis was sayin', Wanda wasn't ready to hear, and that doesn't happen often. She was always on top of everything, always in control. It's one of the things I admired most about her. I thought for a minute about how I enjoyed listening to Wanda order her staff around. I like strong women. Women like Cassandra and Wanda.

And if that's true, why do I gravitate toward women like Mystique and Jacara?

"Okay, Glynnis. I understand completely," Wanda said and began nodding her head as Glynnis talked. It was what Glynnis was best at: talking. That's why I liked Glynnis. If it had anything to do with politics and power, she was all over it. She wasn't a bad-lookin' woman, just not my type.

Wanda pressed end on her phone and looked at me. "Glynnis doesn't want to talk on the phone. She said she wants to meet you in an hour at a place called Soul Fixin's. It's on Thirty-fourth."

"You heard the lady, driver," I said to Bobby.

"Fuck you," was his response, but he headed for the Midtown Tunnel and we were there waiting at the restaurant when Glynnis walked up. After she ordered a cup of coffee, she and I walked down Thirty-fourth, with Bobby and Wanda following behind.

"I'm sorry to be going through all this with you, but I really don't want to be involved. But I have to tell you this, I just don't want anything to happen to me," she said, and her hand shook a little as she sipped her coffee.

"Nothin' gonna happen to you, Glynnis. I promise you that. I would never let anything happen to you. Just tell me what you gotta tell me. It will be all right."

"I was at a party last night and I overheard a conversation between Martin Marshall and his man, Scotty. I heard Martin say, if Mike Black ever found out I had any involvement in his wife's murder, he'll kill us all."

Chapter 18

Mike Black

Martin Marshall was a state senator that I had done business with a few times. But he was such a greedy fuck that I had to cut him loose years ago. Since we had no business ties, I couldn't imagine how he would be involved in Cassandra's murder, but I would find out. We dropped Wanda off at her house and me and Bobby went to see Marshall at his house.

On the way there I thought about Martin and his connection to Diego Estabon. I knew that the two of them were involved, but I didn't know how deep it was. The two of them were involved in the death of a reporter named Tavia Hawkins. I gave the information to Kirk and I figured that would be punishment enough, but Martin Marshall wouldn't go down that easy. Martin got immunity from prosecution for testifying against some congressmen in Brooklyn over a real estate development and walked away clean.

None of this was making any sense to me. How could Diego be involved in Cassandra's murder? When it first happened, Diego was one of the first people I thought of. But I quickly eliminated him because of the way things were goin'. The same logic still applied. If Diego or even his father, Gomez, wanted to kill Cassandra and kill me in jail they wouldn't have hired Bart or his boy, Swan, when there are plenty of homeboys, both in and out of jail that they could have tapped to do the job.

It just didn't make sense.

I decided then that I wasn't going to Hong Kong, at least for the time being. There was enough goin' on right here that seemed more promising than running around Hong Kong chasing the wild goose. I didn't think that Martin was responsible for, or too deeply involved, in Cassandra's murder; he was too much of a punk, but you never know. I was hopeful that whatever he knew would lead me to the people responsible. Maybe then Cassandra could rest peacefully, and maybe then I could move on with my life.

"We're not going to Hong Kong," I finally informed Bobby.

"I didn't think so. You think Marty knows anything?"

"Maybe," I said simply. I wanted to kill somebody and I didn't think Martin Marshall was the one, so I couldn't get too excited. I reached in my pocket and pulled out a dollar. "Let me use your phone."

"Very funny," Bobby said and practically threw

his cell at me. "I was wondering how long it would take."

"Take for what?" I asked as I punched in the number.

"How long after you decided not to go to Hong Kong would it take for you to call Mystique."

"Who said I was callin' her?"

"Nobody." Bobby smiled. "Go ahead, press talk."

"Huh?"

"When you want to make a call you gotta press the talk button."

"I know that."

"I know you know. Shit, as much as you're on it you should pay the bill."

"I gave you a dollar."

"And I told you that wasn't the point. The point is even though you claim to not like them, that you don't like being that accessible, you have no problem using somebody else's cell phone. You might as well break down, join the new millennium, and get your own. And in case you haven't noticed, you still haven't pressed talk."

"Okay, so I'm callin' Mystique. What's wrong with that?" I asked, and waited for the verbal onslaught that would be Bobby's response.

"Nothin' at all. All I'm sayin' is that like it or not, you're a single man now. You supposed to be fuckin' Mystique's brains out. Her and a whole bunch more. That's all I'm sayin'," Bobby said and kept driving, but it didn't stop there. "You came back from the land of half-naked hoes, but did you at least meet one?"

"There was one."

"Did you fuck her or were you out hidin' behind Michelle?"

"No, I wasn't hidin' behind Michelle. Jamaica introduced me to her and no, I didn't fuck her."

"Why not?" Bobby asked louder than he needed to.

I wasn't about to tell him that she practically set it out for me, but that I ran off the island. "I didn't have time. I wanted to get back here so we could leave for Hong Kong," I lied, but it was one that he couldn't dispute.

"So who is she? And don't tell me that it was that fine-ass muthafucka that does the show that he's always talkin' 'bout. If that's who it is, I don't even want to hear about it."

"Okay." I finally pressed talk.

"Is it her?"

I didn't answer.

"Why didn't you fuck her?"

"I told you, I didn't have time," I said as Mystique answered. "It's Black, how you doin'?"

"Better now," Mystique said and I could hear her smile. "I didn't think that I would hear from you so soon."

"Did I catch you at a bad time?"

"No. I wasn't doin' anything," she said quickly. "So, what's Hong Kong like?"

"I haven't left yet."

"Oh, really? I thought you said you were goin' there from the Bahamas?"

"Yeah, but something came up."

"So, where are you?"

"I'm in New York. I just got back this afternoon."

"Well, like I said, I'm not doin' anything other than layin' here naked, gettin' wet thinkin' about you inside me."

"Hold that thought. I got to go see somebody now and you know how one thing always leads to another, so it's gonna be a while, but I'm comin' for you."

"It'll be drippin' wet by that time," Mystique said to me and I could see her layin' there.

"You know that's how I like it."

"If I'm not here, you know where to find me," Mystique said and I knew she meant she'd be at Cynt's. She was all about makin' that money.

"Remind me that we need to talk about that."

"What? Me workin' at Cynt's?"

"Yeah." I was fuckin' her and everybody knows I'm fuckin' her. And since I intended to keep on fuckin' her, that meant she didn't need to be workin' in the club. I would have to find her something else to do; something legit.

"Okay, baby," Mystique said.

"We'll talk soon."

"Very soon, I hope."

I ended the call and handed the phone back to Bobby.

"Now that's what I'm talkin' about. Hit her, drop her off, and let the next nigga get her," he cheered.

"I'm glad you're happy."

"Now tell me about the woman Jamaica is always ravin' 'bout. Is she as fine as he says?" Bobby asked as he parked in front of Martin Marshall's house.

"I don't know what he said about her, but she is a nice package," I said and got out of the car.

Bobby and I walked up to the front door and rang the bell. When his maid answered, Bobby pushed his way past her. "We're here to see Mr. Marshall, sweetie," he said.

"Wait just a minute! You can't just walk in here like you own the place!" the maid screamed at us.

"But that is what we're doin'," Bobby said and I followed behind him. I had been there a few times for parties and tried to remember where his office was. When Martin came out to see what all the noise was about, we walked quickly toward him. When he saw us coming, Martin went back in his office and Bobby and I both took out our guns.

"Oh shit!" the maid yelled and ran behind us.

When the three of us got to Martin's office, we found him standing in front of his bar. "Rémy, isn't it, Black?" he asked and calmly poured Rémy Martin VSOP into three shot glasses.

"Should I get the police, Mr. Marshall?" the maid asked.

"That won't be necessary, Helena. Mr. Black and I are old friends," Martin said and handed me a glass. "Right, Black?"

"That depends on you, Martin," I said and took my drink.

The maid looked at Martin and then at me and Bobby. "Okay, if you say so. Call if you need anything." She backed out of the room, closing the doors behind her.

"Have a seat, gentlemen," Martin said and handed a drink to Bobby. "There's no need for guns. I'm sure if you planned on killing me, I'd be dead already."

"The day isn't over yet," Bobby said. "Say or do

the wrong fuckin' thing and Helena will have a mess to clean up."

Bobby and I sat down and Martin went and sat behind his desk, but neither of us put away our guns.

"Who killed my wife, Martin?" I asked. I started to point my gun at him when I asked, but I figured just him knowing I would kill him was threat enough. Bobby thought otherwise. He pointed his gun at Martin.

"First off, I want to say that I was sorry to hear about her death, Black. I mean that from the heart."

"Thank you. Now, who killed my wife?"

"I don't know for sure, Black, I swear it."

"What do you know?"

"You ever hear of a DEA agent," Martin paused. "Well ex-DEA agent now. Fellow named Kenneth DeFrancisco?"

"No."

"I was in business with him and Diego Estaban."

"I knew about you and Diego. What was the setup?"

"Same old same. Diego brings it in, DeFrancisco was responsible for security, and I provided whatever political cover they needed."

"What does this have to do with my wife, Martin?"

"Diego got careless; let some DEA operative compile some major document on his operation. It was only by chance that DeFrancisco got wind of an ongoing South American operation and mentioned the details that he'd heard that Diego knew he had a snitch."

"Interesting story, Martin, but the man asked you about his wife," Bobby said.

"That's what I'm doing," Martin said nervously as he looked at Bobby's gun. "That's why Diego tried to set up you and his father."

"I know all this, Martin. Tell me about my wife."

"That's what I'm doing. When it all fell apart, DeFrancisco went to jail. He's doin' time at the federal pen in Atlanta. Since he's been there, he's been reaching out to me to use my influence to get him moved to a minimum-security facility, but I can't help him. Too much bad will out there for him. He stepped on a lot of people."

"I'm gettin' bored, Martin," Bobby advised him. "And when that happens my finger might slip," he warned, and I wanted to laugh at how corny that was, but I kept my game face on.

"Okay, okay. Last week his lapdog, Vinnelli, comes to see me," Martin continued.

"Who's he?" I asked.

"DEA. He tells me that DeFrancisco wants to talk to me and if I don't, DeFrancisco would start remembering things. So I called him."

"What did he want?"

"Same thing. Get him transferred to a minimum-security facility. Said if I didn't get it done soon, that the same thing that happened to your wife would happen to mine."

"You think he really meant he had her killed, or was he just tryin' to scare you?" Bobby asked, and I started thinking about how I was gonna kill that muthafucka.

"I asked him if he was responsible for that and

he just gave me that look, you know." Martin looked at me. "You gonna kill me, Black?"

"Not yet," I told him. "There's something that I want you to do for me first."

Chapter 19

Kirk and Richards returned to Cash Money's murder scene to have a second look, as they usually did. Especially when they didn't have too much to go on. Revisiting the scene gave Kirk a fresh opportunity to think through the murder and see what they might have missed the first time. "There's always something," Kirk was famous for saying at these occasions. This time was no different.

Since they had come to the conclusion that the murder of Cash Money and K Murder were related, Kirk and Richards had been to the police impound and looked over K Murder's Escalade, as well as the spot where the shooting took place. Finding no new inspiration, the detectives found themselves at Cash Money's apartment. The results seemed to be the same.

"What now?" Richards asked as they left the apartment.

"I was thinking about grabbing some lunch and then I thought we'd take a another run at this Stark character," Kirk answered.

He had confirmed from his sources that Cash Money Blake, Kevin "K Murder" Murdock, Billy "BB" Banner, and Bruce Stark, all four of Birdie's lieutenants, were members of the Commission. However, his sources told him that the sole purpose of the group was formed to protect themselves against Mike Black. The ability to buy at a cheaper price was nothing more than a by-product.

Even with that information, Kirk was still reluctant to believe that Black was involved with these murders.

When the detectives stopped at a diner for lunch, Richards asked the question he'd been wanting to ask all day. "Why haven't you even suggested, with everything people have been telling us about this commission, why haven't you even suggested we talk to Black, Freeze, or any of his people?" he asked as the waitress placed their meals in front of them.

"Can you bring me another cup of coffee, honey?" Kirk said to the waitress.

"Sure," she replied.

"We can ride out to the country and talk to Black if you want. That's not a problem. But you asked me why I hadn't suggested it, right?"

"Okay, why?"

"Because of what all the people we've talked to haven't told us."

"I'm not following you," Richards said as the waitress returned to refresh Kirk's coffee.

"Thank you, honey."

"Can I get you anything else?" the waitress asked.

"We're fine, thank you," Richards told her and she disappeared.

"What have they been telling us?"

"That after Black had Birdie and Albert killed, these four assholes were so afraid that he'd come after them next, that they formed this commission to protect themselves against him."

"How's that goin' so far?" Kirk asked as he ate.

"Not good. Two of them are dead and the other two are keeping a very low profile."

"Anything else?"

"No, that's pretty much been the story."

"They found Birdie's body near Atlantic City, right? New Jersey state police making any headway with that case?"

"Not that I know of," Richards said.

"But it's assumed that Black killed him and that since nobody's seen his partner, Albert Web, that he's dead too and that Black killed him, right?"

"Right."

"Okay, let's say that Black killed Birdie and Albert. Can you tell me why?"

"Because Black first thought that they killed his wife."

"And you're sure about that? Not sure enough to make an arrest, but sure that's why Black killed or had them killed?"

"I'll go along with that. Yeah, I'm sure about that," Richards answered confidently.

"How come?"

"Because that's what the talk was at the time and why these assholes got together in the first place."

"My point is, what we're not hearing is a reason why Black would be out to kill these guys. And don't give me that crap about him hating all drug dealers. Him and Chilly coexisted for years before Nick killed him. But that wasn't business; Simmons was fuckin' Chilly's wife. No, Pat, I'm not buying it. But like I said, Black is staying out in Rockland County with Bobby Ray and his wife. We can take a ride out there and on the way you can tell me what his motive is, 'cause that's the first thing Black is gonna ask you." Kirk picked up his fork and shoved food in his mouth. "Hey, maybe we'll get lucky and Wanda will be there and you can explain your motive to her."

"You're the one with the thing for her," Richards said. "But I ain't mad at you about it."

"From what everybody tells us, Freeze has been running things quietly and that Black hasn't been seen or heard from much since his wife was murdered. You know as well as I do that he's obsessed with finding her killer. Unless something happened to change that, these four punks wouldn't even be on his radar. And if there was something going on, we'd have heard about it by now."

"What else we got?"

"Nothing," Kirk said. "We have everything to gain and nothing to lose by talking to him."

"Then it's settled. We talk to Stark and then we ride out to see Black," Richards said and Kirk agreed.

It wasn't too long before the detectives found themselves turning down Stark's block. As Richards turned onto the street, Kirk glanced in his side-view mirror and noticed that the young lady who was standing on the corner talking on her cell phone, was now using that cell to take a picture of their car. "Slow down, Pat. I wanna see how they're set up here," Kirk instructed.

"You got it. Slow and steady," Richards said and allowed the car to coast down the street.

"Go around again, then park."

"Yes, sir," Richards said and complied with his partner's request. He drove around the block and came down the street again and parked the car down the street from Stark's building. The stunt had the desired effect, as four of Stark's men approached the car.

"I'm gonna go out on a limb and say he's home this time," Richards said and started to get out of the car.

"Wait," Kirk said quickly and grabbed his arm. "Wait for them to get here."

Just before they got to the car, Kirk and Richards got out with their badges visible. "Is there a problem, gentlemen?" Richards asked and the men stopped.

"No problem, Officer," one said and the others scattered.

"Not so fast," Richards said and walked up to the closest one to him. "Why don't you take us to your scoutmaster?"

"I don't know what you talkin' 'bout."

"Whatever," Richards said and shoved him toward the building. "Go on."

Kirk and Richards were escorted to Stark's apartment, and after waiting five minutes with four of his men, Stark came into the room and sat down.

"I'm Detective Richards and this is Detective Kirkland."

"If you gentlemen don't mind, can I see your credentials, please?" Stark asked and the detectives complied. "Can't be too careful, you know what I mean. Now, what can I do for you?"

"We wanted to ask you some questions about a couple of murders," Richards began.

"You gonna have to be more specific than that," Stark said and smiled. "People get killed around here all the time."

"Look, this can go any way you want it to," the young detective started, but Kirk held up one hand.

"Steven Blake and Kevin Murdock. Anything you can tell me about that?" Kirk asked.

"Can't help you with that, sorry."

"Really?" Kirk said and scratched his head. "Seems to me that help is exactly what you need."

"What you talkin' 'bout?" Stark asked.

"Let's cut the shit, shall we?" Kirk said.

"Let's," Stark said.

"Cash Money and K Murder were members of the Commission, which by the way, you're chairman of. The two of them were murdered, and from what I can see, you have the appearance of a man who's trying to avoid the same fate," Kirk said.

"I don't know what you mean."

"Well, let's see; first there's the girl taking pictures of every car that comes down the street and the two on the far corner. Then there's the four-goon welcoming committee outside the building. There are two men in the lobby and another four in the hallway. Two at the elevator and one at each of the stairwells." Kirk looked over at Richards. "Did I miss anybody?"

Richards glanced around the room. "Other than these four assholes, no, I think you got them all."

"Understand now?"

Stark didn't answer.

"Now, like I was saying, Cash Money and K Murder were murdered and seems to me that you're expecting somebody to come after you. So, who'd you guys piss off?"

"I'm sorry to hear about Cash and K, I really am. But I can't help you. Maybe they got into something that flipped on them and that why they're dead, but it ain't got shit to do with me," Stark said.

"You ever hear of a guy named Mike Black?" Richards asked.

"Sure. What about him?"

"Ever met him?"

"Not personally, but I've seen him around."

"What do think of him?"

"Got nothin' but respect for the man. It's dangerous not to respect Mike Black."

"The way I hear it, you commissioners got together 'cause you were afraid of Black."

"I don't know who you're talkin' to, but I ain't scared of no man," Stark boasted.

Richards looked around the room again. "Yeah, I see why."

Kirk took out a business card and stood up. "If you think of anything that might be helpful, whatever that might be, give me a call," the detective said and left Stark's apartment.

Once they were in the car, Richards turned to Kirk. "What do you think?"

"Even if I don't believe that Black is involved, Stark does, and he doesn't plan on being next. So let's go talk to Black; see what he's got to say."

"It will definitely be more entertaining than this guy," Richards commented and drove off.

Chapter 20

Mike Black

I miss you, Cassandra.

I miss her so much sometimes I can hardly breathe.

I miss everything about her.

I waited my whole life to feel for somebody the way I felt for Cassandra, and now she's dead.

I miss her smile and the way her eyes would dance when she would see me. I miss long conversations about nothing in particular; I just miss talkin' to her.

I long to feel her head against my chest, and feeling the warmth of her body next to mine. I wanna share a meal with her and wonder why it always takes her so long to order. Maybe 'cause she was too busy talkin' instead of looking at the menu. But I love her anyway.

Some days it feels like I'm just walkin' through life, one day to the next. I have nothing to look forward to now. I know she's not going to be there when I get home. I can't call her just to hear that sexy voice of hers. Some days I'm like, what's the point?

Michelle helps a lot with that, 'cause when I look at her, I know I have a purpose. I'm her father. No disrespect to M, but when you get right down to it, I'm all she has in this world. And I won't let her down.

But the only time I really feel alive are times like this. When there's even the slightest possibility that I might find out why my baby had to die. She was the only thing that ever really mattered to me; other than money, I mean. But Cassandra meant more to me than money, 'cause I would gladly give up all the money I have, or ever will have, if there was a chance that I could see her again.

Why somebody had to take that from me, something that good from me, something I've waited all my life for, I don't know. But now I know who, and he will tell me why right before I cut his throat.

When Bobby turned the car off and asked, "You gettin' out or you gonna keep on sittin' there lookin' stupid?" That's when I realized that we were at his house. By the time I got out of the car, Bobby had already taken my bags out of the trunk.

"I know you got a lot on your mind right now. You're thinkin' about why this DeFrank whatever muthafucka had Shy killed. I know you thinkin' about how you gonna kill these muthafuckas, but take a breath," Bobby said and opened the front door.

I followed him inside and downstairs to the basement, which Bobby had claimed as his own personal space. Once he made himself comfortable, he continued. "You thinkin' 'bout killin' two DEA agents?"

"One."

"One what?"

"One DEA. The other one's in jail."

"That presents another set of problems," Bobby said.

"Why, 'cause he's in jail? Bein' in jail don't stop shit. You know that. He can still get got." And Martin Marshall was gonna help me with that. "Being in jail didn't stop him from puttin' a contract on me and Cassandra. No, Bobby, I'm sorry, that muthafucka is gonna die for this."

"And I'm not saying that we couldn't kill them. It ain't like I could stop you anyway."

He had that right.

"All I'm sayin' is to take a breath and think for a minute."

"That's what I'm doin'. I didn't walk out of Marshall's house and wanna go shoot up DEA headquarters, did I?"

"No, that would be stupid."

"Bob, when have you ever known me to rush off and do stupid shit?"

"You never lost your wife before," he reasoned.

What could I say? Bobby was absolutely right. This being about Cassandra did change everything for me, and to be honest, I did think about goin' down to DEA headquarters and shootin' everybody I could find, but I knew it would be suicide—but I thought about it.

When Martin told me that shit, I was on fire. It was all I could do to keep from killin' him. Not 'cause I thought he was more involved in it than he said.

Just because.

Because somebody had to die for this. But I needed Martin Marshall and he would be more useful to me alive. After I got these other two muthafuckas, we'll see how much his life is worth.

"It's not that I'm disagreeing with you, Bobby. I know what I'm thinkin' about doin' could come back on all of us. Kill a DEA agent, and we might have every law enforcement officer in the country comin' down on us."

"I don't know about you, but that's something I want to avoid at all costs."

"And you think I don't?" I asked my best friend.

Bobby just looked at me. "You never lost a wife before. Ain't no tellin' where your head is. I can't even imagine what it must be like for you." Bobby got up and went to the bar to pour us some drinks. "Look man, all I'm sayin' is I'm with you whatever you decide to do. Let's just go slow."

Bobby handed me my drink and I drained the glass. "You should have brought the bottle."

"Like that's a problem."

"First thing we need to do is find out who these fuckas are. I mean everything. I'm not really all that worried about killin' DeFrancisco. Buy the right lifer's family a house and he gets shanked in the shower."

"You can probably get it done cheaper than that," Bobby said.

"I'm just sayin', Bob. He can be done and nobody would care."

"Right, right."

"It's the other muthafucka, this DEA muthafucka, that I'm worried about."

"I didn't know you were back, Mike," Pam said as she came down the steps. Pam and I have always had a special bond. She gave me another year with Cassandra and she is a big help with Michelle.

"We just got here," I told her.

"There are two city cops at the door lookin' for you, Mike. You want me to send them away?"

"City cops?" I questioned.

"Kirk?" Bobby questioned.

"Gotta be," I said and got up. "I got a few answers I want from the good detective."

"You didn't invite them in, did you?" Bobby asked.

"Of course not. They're outside," Pam advised.

"Want me to go out there with you?" Bobby asked as I went up the stairs.

"Just look out for me," I said and was out the door. "Kirk!" I said loudly. On top of my having answers to get from him, I actually liked Kirk. Respected him. I owed my freedom to this man. If it wasn't for Kirk, I'd be doing life for murdering Cassandra. I know it must have been an interesting paradox for him. After all those years of tryin' to lock me up, he goes out of his way to prove that I didn't do it. He doesn't know it, or maybe he does, but I owe him, and it's a debt I had every intention on paying.

I started walking away from the house. "What are you two doin' way out here? And more important, how did you find the place?"

"We did miss that turn a few times," Kirk said

and Richards cracked a smile, something he rarely does in front of me.

Once I was out in the street I stopped and faced the detectives. I wanted to bust right out and ask them what they knew about DeFrancisco and Vinnelli, but I took Bobby's advice and took a deep breath. They came out here for a reason. The best approach was to hear them out on whatever bullshit they had to say and be as cooperative as possible without turning snitch. I hate snitches, 'cause if you'll snitch for me, you'll snitch on me.

But before they left for the city, I would have my answers. "Yeah, that turn is hard to find, especially this time of night; sun setting in your eyes, street signs get hard to read." Neither detective seemed interested in making small talk about traffic patterns. "So what up, Kirk?"

When Kirk looked at Richards and took a step back, I knew that he didn't think whatever Richards was about to ask me was relevant to whatever case they were on. That would make gettin' what I wanted from Kirk that much easier.

"Do you know a Steven Blake or a Kevin Murdock?" Richards asked and handed me two pictures.

I looked at the pictures and handed them back to him. "No, I don't know either of them. Should I?"

"Their street names are Cash Money and K Murder. You ever hear of them?"

"No."

"What about a guy named Stark or Billy Banner, goes by BB?"

"Never heard of any of them. They sound like

cartoon characters to me," I laughed and Kirk chuckled a little, but not Richards. He remained stone-faced like this was important.

"Well, they've heard of you. In fact, they're so worried that you're gonna kill them, that they formed a little group."

"What kind of group?"

"They call themselves the Commission."

"What are they, a rap group or something?" I asked, fighting back the laughter. I glanced over at Kirk and he was doin' the same thing.

"No, they're low-rent drug dealers that used to work for Birdie," Richards said.

"Now him I heard of. Heard they found his body in some river in Jersey," I taunted. "But you answered your own question. If these guys are low-rent drug dealers, I wouldn't know them or anything about them. Maybe you should talk to Freeze. He keeps up with that kind of shit. It's like a hobby to him. But since you drove all the way out here to ask me about them, it must be something that you can only ask me."

"That would be correct," Richards said.

I took a step closer to him. "You don't like me, do you, Detective Richards? To you I'm just another arrogant crook who doesn't deserve the respect Kirk shows me."

"That would be correct," Richards stated plainly.

"That's why I respect you, Detective Richards, 'cause you don't like me and you have no problem lettin' me know that you don't like me. You're not like a lot of other cops who smile in my face or try to act tough. You do your job, and I respect you for that."

"Right," Richards said.

I knew I caught him off guard, but I meant what I said. "Whatever I can do to help you, Detective Richards."

"Somebody killed Cash Money in his apartment and K Murder was killed this weekend in a drive-by."

"I don't know anything about that. I just came back from the Bahamas today. Like I said, Freeze keeps up with that type of shit. So unless you're tellin' me that these are the guys that killed my wife, I wouldn't know anything about them. Why would I?"

"That's what I asked one of them," Richards said.

"What he say?"

"He didn't have a reason either, but right now he's sitting behind fifteen guys—"

"Seventeen," Kirk corrected.

"Okay, seventeen guys; waiting for you to come after him."

"So let me get this straight: four baby ballers that I've never heard of, are so scared that I'm gonna kill them that they get together to protect themselves against me, but I don't know them?" By that time, I couldn't hold back the laughter anymore. "But now two of them are dead, which says a lot for their security and they think it's me that killed them. So now, one of them is so scared of me that he is sittin' behind a little army waitin' on me to show up. Is that what you're tellin' me?"

By then Kirk was laughing too.

Now I have a decision to make and it's not gonna be easy. What about Michelle? Leaving her here for a couple of weeks while I went to Hong Kong with Bobby was one thing, but the assassination attempt changes all that. If I left her in Freeport with my mother, Emily, would she be safe? Or would somebody come to kill her like they did her mother? I couldn't be sure of that either.

"What's up, Jamaica?" I said and shook his hand. His real name was Clyde Walker, but we've always called him Jamaica since the day he got off the banana barge and moved on our block.

"Ain't nuthin', rude boy. It's good to see you," Jamaica said while he smiled and poked fun at Michelle. She laughed a little and smiled at Jamaica and I knew it wouldn't be long before she had him eating out of her hand too. "Come, me have a car waitin'."

"You bring a car seat for Michelle?"

"Yes, sir. Me pick it out personally," he said and continued to flirt with Michelle.

"You bring enough people with you?" I asked as we walked to the parking lot surrounded by his men.

"Somebody try to kill you. Maybe they try again here," Jamaica said.

"I can't argue with your logic."

"You have any idea who it was?" Jamaica asked.

"No."

"Me know you must tink same people involved with kill Cassandra."

"Yeah, but who are they? To be honest with you, I hope it is. Gives me one more reason to cut their fuckin' hearts out. But I really don't know if this is connected or if this is some other shit. Me and Bobby are goin' to Hong Kong when I get back to the city."

"What's in Hong Kong?"

"Another wild goose probably," I said, because that's how it felt sometimes, but I gotta check it out.

"You leave the baby with M?" Jamaica asked. It was Cassandra who had tagged my mother with the name *M* after we watched *Die Another Day*. Cassandra said that my mother was the same type of strong, no-nonsense woman that Judi Dench now plays as head of the British secret service.

"That right, so I don't care what M says, I want you to double the men you got on the house."

"It's done."

"I'm trustin' you with my girls, J. I'm holdin' you personally responsible for their safety."

"Me die before I allow one hair 'pon she head to be harmed," Jamaica said and continued teasing with Michelle.

"Here, you wanna hold her?" I asked and handed her to him without waiting for an answer. He was a little awkward with her at first, but he settled down once Michelle smiled at him.

When Cassandra and I left New York and moved to Freeport, Jamaica became the houseguest who just wouldn't leave, but I wasn't rushin' him to go. After we killed André Harmon, Jamaica disappeared and I didn't see him for years. During that time he got hooked on heroin and at that time he had just kicked it. As far as Cassandra and I were concerned, he could stay as long as he needed or wanted to.

As he began to feel better and his mind got clearer, Jamaica began moving around, seeing how things worked on the island. Shootin' craps was big on the island, but the locals couldn't gamble in the casinos. It didn't take him long to take over those independent games and set up new ones. Once that was organized and running smooth, I had Jamaica turn his attention to extortion. He began shaking down anybody who made money on the tourist industry. From tour operators, to bus and cab companies. From the guys who took tourists out on their boats on fishing trips, to the port merchants. If you made money, we made money.

When we got to my house, there were another two of Jamaica's men waiting for us. He always rotated two men to look out for my mother so one of them would be with her at all times. My mother didn't like having them around. She didn't allow them in the house and only acknowledged their presence when she needed them, but she'd gotten used to it. Since there were two of them there, I could only assume he had already stepped up security. Under the circumstances I couldn't argue with his logic.

I had been there for a couple of days, enjoying my mother and watching her enjoy Michelle. The first day was a little rough startin' out for the girls. M had only seen Michelle twice before that. The first time was just after she was born and again after Cassandra died. And with Michelle not likin' women, she screamed bloody murder every time M tried to pick her up. "What is wrong with this child, Michael?" M had asked that first day.

"She doesn't like women. She barely tolerates Pam holding her."

"I can barely tolerate Pam," M said and tried to walk Michelle to quiet her. "I don't like her. I thought she was just ignorant, now to find out that she's crazy too." M gave me that look that I hated to see when I was a kid. "And this is the woman you got raising my grandbaby? I just don't understand you sometimes, Michael," she yelled over Michelle's screaming. I stood up and took Michelle from her. She got very quiet and M rolled her eyes at me.

"That baby needs a home, Michael."

"She has a home."

"Really, where?"

"We live at Bobby's house," I said, even though I knew what she meant. We have had this conversation before, and it always goes the same way.

"Don't get smart with me, Michael. You need a home of your own. It's time for you to stop hiding out at Bobby's house and move on with your life. I'm sure Cassandra wouldn't want this life for you and this precious baby," M said and took Michelle from my arms.

She immediately went into her act. M gave Michelle the look. "You listen to me, young lady. I am your grandmother and I will not have you crying your head off every time I touch you. Do you understand me, young lady? You are not wet, your daddy just fed you, so I know you're not hungry. Now you are gonna stop all this foolishness. You hear me?" M had told her granddaughter in the way Cassandra used to and Michelle slowly calmed down. Since that moment, M and Michelle have been all right with each other.

"I'm sorry, but would you mind tellin' me what my motive is for doing this?"

"See, I told you he was going to ask you that," Kirk said and dropped his head to continue getting his laugh on.

"I'm not out there fightin' over corners with these kids," I said before Richards could say anything. "They play it a little too hard for me. They have no honor or loyalty; shootin' each other over bullshit. Why would I even be involved with these guys?"

It didn't take long before Richards cracked a smile. "I was kinda hopin' that you could tell us," he finally said. "Since they think it's all about you, I just thought I'd ask."

"It is not about me, believe that." But now things were starting to make sense. Now I know it was these assholes that sent somebody to kill me.

"I'm sorry we took up your time," Kirk said and turned toward the car.

"Before you go, Kirk. Have you heard anything new you want to share about my wife's murder?"

"I'm sorry to say that there isn't any new information, but believe me, we're still on it," Kirk said.

"And you still don't think you can tell me what you do know about Cassandra's murder?"

"We've been through this before, Black. That would come under the heading of police business."

"Yeah, you told me." I looked at Kirk and then turned to Richards. "Would you excuse us for a minute, Detective Richards?"

Richards extended his hand graciously and I walked away with Kirk. What I was about to do was risky. Some might even say it was arrogant, but it wouldn't be the first time I've been accused of that. I stopped and faced the detective.

"Does the name DeFrancisco mean anything to you?"

The *oh shit* look on Kirk's face answered all the questions I had. This muthafucka killed my baby.

"We've met," was all Kirk would commit to. It wasn't like I expected him to spill his guts and tell me everything he knew, like they do on TV.

"See, I've always believed that you've known who had killed Cassandra for a long time, but there was some reason you couldn't do anything about it. Now I understand some of why that may have been. Here's the problem, Kirk. I know DeFrancisco had her killed and you know what I'm gonna do about it."

"I do."

"The question between you and I is, when I do what I'm gonna do, what are you going to do about it?"

"I'm gonna do my job, Black. I'm gonna follow the evidence whereever it leads. If I didn't do my job, you wouldn't respect me," Kirk explained, and I understood and could respect that. "Just like if you didn't do your job, I wouldn't respect you." Kirk took a step closer to me. "Just make sure you do your best work," he said and left me standing there. "Come on, Pat."

"What was that about?" I heard Richards ask.

"Friend of his got some parking tickets, you know the rest," Kirk said and got in the car.

Chapter 21

Black stood outside the house and watched the detectives drive away. He had just taken a risk by telling Kirk that he knew DeFrancisco was the one who had Shy killed, but it was necessary. And it wasn't all that risky anyway. Black understood that DeFrancisco being found dead in his cell wouldn't be a big deal. The real issue, the one Black didn't mention, was Vinnelli. He was an active DEA agent. His murder would have every law enforcement officer in the country coming after them, and as Bobby said, that's something Black wanted to avoid at all costs.

Black knew that once Kirk heard that Vinnelli was dead, no matter the circumstances, he'd suspect that Black was at least involved, if he didn't do the job personally. At that point, Kirk would do his job, but Black felt like he had an understanding with Kirk. He would follow the evidence. "Just make sure you do your best work," was what Kirk told him. Black took that to mean that there couldn't be any evidence of his involvement in Vinnelli's death.

Black went back in the house where Bobby was waiting with Pam. "Come on, we need to ride," Black said to Bobby and walked back out.

Bobby stood up and followed him out.

Pam came out behind him. "What goin' on, Mike?"

"Nothin' for you to be worried about," Black said and got in the car.

Bobby kissed his wife on the cheek. "I'll be back as soon as I can. By the way, we're not goin' to Hong Kong," he said and got in the car.

"We got more problems," Black said before Bobby could shut his door. "Let me see your phone." Bobby handed Black the phone without discussion.

He dialed Freeze's number and he answered quickly. "What's up?"

"I need to see you, Nick, and Wanda. I'm at Bobby's. We're on our way to the city."

"Where you wanna meet?"

"Cynt's," Black replied and Bobby started laughing. Black gave Bobby the finger and ended the call.

"What they want?" Bobby asked.

"You ever hear of some baby ballers go by the names Cash Money and K Murder?"

"Nope."

"They're dead."

"So?"

"They wanted to know if I killed them."

"Did you?"

"I never even heard of these kids. But them two, and two others that used to work for Birdie, formed a group they call the Commission to protect themselves against me."

Bobby started laughing. "You're kidding."

"I'm serious, Bobby. It was probably them who sent that muthafucka to kill me."

"You're probably right. Now what we gonna do about it?"

"Shit—you know we gonna pay them a visit."

"Say good-bye," Bobby laughed as he drove into the city.

When he and Black walked in Cynt's, Nick, Freeze, and Wanda were waiting for them. As Black approached the table that they were seated at, he looked around the room for Mystique, but didn't see her anywhere.

When the trio saw Black and Bobby coming, they stood up. Freeze walked up to Black. "You wanna talk in Cynt's office?"

"No. I need the noise."

"Cool," Freeze said and smiled because he knew Black wanted to talk about killing somebody. He looked at Black as he shook Nick's hand and hugged Wanda. He saw the fire in Black's eyes. The kind of fire he hadn't seen since he buried Shy.

Black sat down and got right to it. "Any of you heard anything 'bout some niggas call themselves the Commission?" Black asked over the music.

"No," Freeze said flatly and Nick and Wanda both shook their heads. Nick glanced at Wanda, who was going out of her way not to look in his direction.

"What about Cash Money or K Murder?"

"Yeah," Freeze said. "I heard Cash and a couple of his boyz got killed."

"The other nigga got killed a couple of days ago."

"What about them, Mike?" Wanda asked, knowing if Black was asking about two dead drug dealers, it couldn't be good.

"Kirk and Richards just asked me if I was involved. Before you get excited, it ended with us all having a big laugh about it."

"Where did you see Kirk?" Wanda needed to know.

"At Bobby's house."

"You're tellin' me that two New York City detectives drove all the way out to Bobby's house to ask you about two murders and it's no big deal?" Wanda asked.

"Yeah."

"I'll look into it."

"Thank you, Wanda." Black turned his attention back to Freeze. "Richards says they were part of this commission and they both worked for Birdie. Anybody else you can think of that might be a part of this crew?"

"Stark would definitely be on that team, probably runnin' it," Freeze said.

"Do I even know this nigga?"

"I don't think so," Freeze said.

"What you got to do with them?" Nick asked.

Black took his time and explained the Commission and its purpose. When he was though, everybody was laughing. "That's probably who tried to get you in the bathroom, Freeze," Nick said.

"What? What happened in the bathroom?" Bobby asked. "Somebody try to get a piece of that ass?" he said, still laughing.

"The other night me and Freeze were out tryin' to find out who came after you and three guys followed him in the bathroom."

"To kill me, " Freeze said quickly.

"What happened?" Black asked, no longer laughing.

"I got two of them, Freeze got the other," Nick told him.

"When were y'all gonna tell me about this?"

"You said you didn't wanna hear day-to-day shit like that," Freeze answered.

"You're right. I did. But I don't think somebody tryin' to kill y'all while you're out tryin' to find out who tried to kill me is more than day-to-day shit." Black glared at Wanda. "You know about this?"

Wanda looked at Freeze and then at Nick. "This is the first I'm hearing about this too," Wanda said, still staring at Nick and wondering why he didn't tell her before turning back to Black. "Nobody tells me anything anymore," she spit out angrily. "How'd you leave it?"

Freeze laughed a little. "We left them dead in the bathroom."

"Anybody see you leaving?" Wanda asked.

"Anybody who was looking," Freeze said. "But my people say the cops ain't up on us."

Black thought for a minute. "So somebody hit Cash, they think it's me and send somebody to get me. I kill him and they send three guys after you."

"They probably think we killed this other muthafucka to retaliate," Nick said.

"That means that they're gonna be comin' at us again," Freeze said. "What do you wanna do, Black?"

"I wanna find and kill whoever it was that murdered Cassandra," Black said and looked at Bobby. "None of this other bullshit matters to me right now. You command this family now. You handle this shit, but I wanna know what's goin' on; understand?"

"Yes, sir," Freeze replied. He understood that that meant he shouldn't do anything without talking to Black first.

"You and Bobby still goin' to Hong Kong?" Nick asked.

"No."

Wanda stood up and looked at Freeze. "Unless you need me for anything else, I'm going home."

"I do want you to check on Kirk; see if they really got anything they think connects Black to this. Like you said, they didn't just ride all the way to Bobby's house for nothing."

"Yes, sir," Wanda said and saluted. "Mike, give me a call and let me know what Marshall had to say."

"We'll talk in the morning. There's somethin' I wanna run by you. What time is good for you, Counselor?"

"I'll be home all day, stop by anytime. We need to talk about something," Wanda said, thinking about telling him about her and Nick. Lately she'd been thinking that it would be better if she told him than Black finding out on his own. "Good night, gentlemen." Wanda looked at Nick and walked away. She knew this meant she would be spending another night alone. Wanda understood the reason why and understood it was necessary, but she didn't have to like it.

Nick stood up and was about to follow Wanda. He could tell by the look she gave him that she was not happy. This was the first time he'd seen her in a couple of days and he wanted to at least spend a few minutes with her before him and Freeze got in the street. "I'll get with you later, Freeze. I got something I need to take care of."

"Sit down, Nick. I need to talk to you," Black said and Nick quickly reclaimed his seat. "You too, Freeze."

"What's up?" Nick asked.

"You ever met or hear of a DEA agent named DeFrancisco, or one named Vinnelli, Nick?"

"Not that I can remember, why?"

"Defrancisco had Cassandra killed. I want you to find out everything you can about these two muthafuckas. DeFrancisco is in jail; find out where."

"I'm on it."

"The one that I'm concerned with is Vinnelli. He's probably the one who set things in motion. Get on top of him. I want to know the cleanest way to take him."

"You plannin' on killin' a DEA agent, Black?" Nick asked.

"Yeah, I am." Black looked at Freeze. "You wanna ask me that shit too? Hell yeah, I'm gonna kill him and every fuckin' body I think was down with it. These the muthafuckas that killed Cassandra, these the muthafuckas that are gonna die for it!"

"He just askin' a question, Mike," Bobby said

calmly. "Same question I asked you. We all with you, you know that. It's just a question."

"All right, all right," Black spit out.

"I understand this is personal to you, like I said, I'm on it," Nick promised. "Say the word and he'll be dead tomorrow."

"You tell me how and we'll see," Black said and noticed that Mystique had come into the room. She smiled when she saw him looking at her. "But I wanna go slow with this. Make sure nothin' comes back on us. Whether y'all believe me or not, I don't plan on goin' to jail, so we take our time and do this right. That's it, Nick. I know you got shit to do."

Nick stood up. "I'll get on this right away. I'll get with you later, Freeze."

"Whatever, Nick," Freeze said and knew Nick was going to see Wanda, so it would be much later.

"Freeze," Black said as Nick left Cynt's.

"Yeah?"

"Wanda is fuckin' somebody, you know anything about that?"

"Nope," Freeze lied.

"I wanna know who he is."

"What you want me to do when I find him?"

"Nothin'. I'll kill him myself. Now, tell me about this nigga, Stark."

Mystique waited patiently for Black to get finished talking, even though she wanted desperately to go over there and tell Freeze and Bobby that they'd had enough time with her man and now it was her turn. As much as she wanted to, Mystique knew that it wouldn't be a good idea. She could tell something was up when she got to Cynt's and saw Freeze and Nick with him. Usually when Black came there, it would just be him and Bobby—*Who seems like he's on a mission to fuck every trickin' ho that worked at Cynt's,* Mystique thought as she watched Black. She loved looking at him so much that at times she couldn't stop herself. He was so handsome and his eyes were so intense. *And that sexy-ass voice; I love listening to my man talk.*

Her man?

Mystique knew it was stupid, but she was falling in love with Mike Black. Whether he felt anything for her or not, Mike Black was her man. She had something none of the other hoes there had and so many wanted. *When he walks in every jealous-ass bitch in this joint knows he's here to see me. They all know he is my man,* Mystique thought as Black got up and started coming in her direction.

"Hey, handsome," Mystique said and touched his face. Something else she loved doing.

"What's up with you?"

"I'm fine."

"I know. How's your night?"

Mystique looked around the room. "Well, you know I just got here, and from the looks of things, it's gonna be a slow night."

"I know you just got here, I saw you when you came in. But I asked about your night. The night didn't begin when you got here, or is this all there is for you?"

"No, this isn't all there is for me, but I am hopin' that my night is just beginning."

Black looked at Mystique without commenting

on what she said. "Come here. Let me talk to you for a minute," he said and took Mystique by the hand and led her up the stairs to Cynt's office.

Black knocked on the door, and not getting an answer, let himself in. "I want to ask you something," Black started, but Mystique had other ideas.

She threw her arms around his neck and forced her tongue down his throat. "I missed you, baby," Mystique said when she stopped to take a breath.

Black looked in Mystique's eyes and thought about the part she played in his decision not to see Jacara that night at the Sheraton and leave the island. "I missed you too."

Mystique got wet hearing those words coming from him. "Whew." She took a step back from him. "What do you want to ask me?"

Black leaned against Cynt's desk and folded his arms across his chest. "Do you like working here?"

"I like the money."

"You could do other things for money."

"Sure I could," Mystique said, smiling inside in anticipation of where Black was going with this. She wanted to say, *but if you want me to stop shakin' "your" ass in here every night I will quit tonight,* but she didn't want to get ahead of herself. "I would much rather train, but I don't have enough clients yet to replace this money."

"You let me worry about money."

"So what are you sayin'?"

"You know what I'm sayin'."

"Yeah, I do," Mystique said and stepped to his chest. "But I wanna hear you say it."

"Mystique! You don't work here anymore. I'll

compensate Cynt for her loss of income, but you don't work here anymore."

His words were music to her ears. Maybe he didn't say I love you, but he definitely stepped up to the plate and claimed her. Mystique couldn't have been happier. "Are we leaving, now?"

"No. I got something to do."

"You found out who killed your wife, didn't you?"

Black looked at Mystique. "Never ask me about my business. The less you know about what I do, the better it is for you."

"I understand. When will I see you again?"

"I don't know. You go home and I'll call you later."

"Yes, baby."

With that said and done, Black and Mystique walked out of the office. As she made her way through the club to the dressing room, she saw Black stop and talk to Cynt before leaving with Bobby.

"Guess you'll be leavin' soon, huh?" one of her haters said.

"Yeah, and I won't be back."

"What?"

"My man don't want me dancin' here no more," Mystique said, smiling, and went to change clothes at Cynt's for the last time.

Chapter 22

"Where we going?" Bobby asked.

"Stark hunting," Black said as he got in the car.

"I thought you told Freeze to handle that?"

"I changed my mind. Why? You got something to do?"

"Nope."

Black and Bobby had been riding for hours, checking out all of the spots Freeze said Stark hung out at. By two in the morning, Bobby had had enough.

"Don't you wanna go back to Cynt's and pick up amazon Shy and call it a night? This nigga gone underground hidin' from you."

"Yeah, you're right. I just wanna roll by one more spot then we'll call it a night. Ride up White Plains Road," Black instructed.

As the two drove down the street, they passed by one of the spots that Freeze told them that Stark frequented. They saw a familiar car. "Isn't that Angelo's car?" Black asked.

"Looks like somebody got a case of jungle fever tonight," Bobby replied, knowing Angelo Collette's fondness for black women.

"That or somebody's gonna die tonight," Black speculated. Bobby parked the car and he and Black went inside.

"Told you," Bobby said when he saw Angelo standing at the bar talking to the most beautiful woman in the place. He walked up behind Angelo and tapped him on the shoulder. "Hey, what you all up in my woman's face for?"

Angelo turned around slowly and smiled when he saw who it was. "Look at what we have here?" Angelo said and turned to his female companion. "Honey, I want you to meet the dynamic duo. This is Batman," he said and pointed to Black. "And this is—"

"If you call me Robin, I'll shoot you right now," Bobby said and made a move for his gun.

"All right, all right. Honey, this is Bobby Ray and Mr. Happy here is Mike Black."

"So, you're Mike Black?" the woman asked.

"You know this guy?" Angelo asked her.

"You can't be from around here and not hear of Mike Black. A friend of mine used to talk about you all the time," she said and looked at Black like she was willing to go with him any time or place to give him a taste.

"I'm glad you're here, Mikey," Angelo said before Black could ask the beautiful woman who her friend was. "Freeze tell you I needed to talk to you?"

"No," Black said, still looking at the woman. She had the type of body that he liked to play with. "I just left Freeze a couple of hours ago, but he didn't mention it. But we're up on something else right now."

"Yeah, he told me. But let me holla at you for a minute, Mikey. Excuse us for a minute, honey. I need to talk to this guy."

"Sure," was her reply.

"It was nice meeting you, Miss—" Black said.

"Cameisha, Cameisha Collins, but you can call me CeCe," she said. Until a few weeks ago, CeCe was Cash Money's woman, but now she was a free agent and looking for a new love. Mike Black would do her nicely, she thought, and watched him walk away.

"What's up, Angee?" Black asked as soon as they were far enough away from CeCe.

"Crazy Joe got out the joint a couple of weeks ago," Angelo said. Joey Delfino used to do jobs with Angelo back in the day. Him, Angelo, and Black were supposed to hijack a load of cigarettes from a truck at the Molly Pitcher service area on the New Jersey Turnpike. Black and Angelo never showed up, so Crazy Joe did the job alone. He was arrested by Newark police at the tollbooth when he got off the Turnpike.

Joey found out later that Black and Angelo were late because on the way to the job, they stopped to rob a jewelry store to settle an argument.

"I ain't scared of shit, Mikey. You fuckin' know that shit," Angelo boasted as they drove to New Jersey to meet Joey.

"All I'm sayin' is I like to plan a job before I do it. That don't make me scared; that makes me careful," Black told Angelo that day.

"You won't do it 'cause you're scared, Mikey. Scared 'cause you don't know what you're walkin' into. Me, I don't give a fuck. I'm ready for whatever they got in there."

"Fuck you, Angee. And fuck that dumb shit you talkin'. We just passed a jewelry store 'bout a block ago. If you such a bad muthafucka, turn this car around and go rob the muthafucka."

"Never challenge me, Mikey. You know better than that shit. You know I will turn this heap around and do that shit, but we gotta meet Crazy Joe."

"What's that I smell? Is it pussy I smell in here? 'Cause it sounds to me like somebody's scared," Black taunted.

"I ain't scared of shit, Mikey, and I ain't no fuckin' pussy," Angelo said and made a U-turn. Angelo double-parked the car in front of the store. "You comin' with me, chickenshit?"

Black put on his gloves. "Let's go," and got out of the car. The robbery went off without any problems, but they got stuck in traffic coming across the George Washington Bridge. When they got to the service area they found Joey's car, but no Joey. Angelo found out the next day that Joey was arrested.

"You talk to him since he got out?" Black asked Angelo, thinking that he already had enough shit to deal with.

"Yeah, I seen him a couple of times."

"What's he talkin' 'bout?"

"Same shit. Still talkin' 'bout killin' you. He says it was your fault 'cause you shouldn't have challenged me and he's got a point," Angelo said.

"Whatever, Angee. It ain't my fault that he went and did the shit by himself. He could have waited for us. That shit didn't make no fuckin' sense."

"We don't call him Crazy Joe for nothing. Anyway, when Freeze said somebody tried to whack you, I asked was the guy black or white. When he said the guy was black, I knew it wasn't Joey," Angelo said.

"No, he'd wanna do the shit himself," Black said. "I know who tried to kill me."

"Who?"

"You ever hear of the Commission?"

"No."

"Whoever they are they thinks I'm out to get them and that I killed some baby baller named Cash Money and some other cartoon-character-soundin' muthafucka."

"I never heard of no commission, but Cash Money, him I heard of. In fact, that used to be his woman," Angelo said and pointed at CeCe.

"No shit," Black said and looked at her on the dance floor. "She seems to be takin' his death well."

"Seemed to me that she was more interested in replacin' him than mourning his death, if you know what I'm sayin'."

"Mind if I take a run at her?"

"What are you, kiddin' me? This is America; it's a free country, Mikey."

"You can have her back when I'm done. I'm not

hiring right now. I'll catch up with you later, Angee," Black said and made his way to the dance floor. He stood in a spot where CeCe could see him. When Black had her attention, he motioned for her to come to him.

CeCe leaned close to her dance partner and whispered something to him. Then she left him standing there and walked straight to Black. "Hello again," CeCe said over the music and stepped closer to him. So close that Black felt her nipples brush against him.

"I need to talk to you."

"What do you want to talk about, baby?"

"Cash."

"The man or the paper?"

"The man."

"I would much rather talk to you about something else, but I figured that's what you wanted. What you wanna know?"

"Where can I find Stark?"

"Why, so you can kill him too?" CeCe asked.

"Let's get something straight. I never even heard of these niggas and their commission before tonight."

"Then why they think you killed Cash and K?"

"I have no fuckin' idea. I'm lookin' for Stark to settle this shit. I am not his enemy. You tell him that for me. Tell him I wanna sit down with him, 'cause we ain't got no problems."

"I'll tell him next time I talk to him."

"You do that," Black said and started to walk away, but CeCe grabbed his arm.

"How can I get in touch with you?" CeCe asked.

"Why you wanna get in touch with me?"

"In case Stark wanna meet."

"He'll know how to get in touch with me."

"Okay. Suppose I wanted to get in touch with you?"

"Why you wanna get in touch with me?"

" 'Cause I like the way you was lookin' at me before you found out I was with Cash. I could tell you wanted me."

"Is that right?"

"That's right. So, I was thinkin' maybe you and I could get together sometime."

"How would I know you wouldn't be settin' me up as revenge for killin' your man?"

"You wouldn't. But me and Cash wasn't that deep. I had only been with him for a couple of months. The truth is, I just liked what he was doin' for me."

"I can get to that. A woman gotta do what a woman gotta do," Black said to CeCe. She was right about one thing, he had thought about seeing her naked before he found out she was with Cash. "You just tell Stark what I said. Once this is settled, maybe I'll get with you."

"How will you find me?" CeCe asked.

"Don't worry, I'll find you when I want you," Black said and left her standing there.

Once he found Bobby, the two left the club and headed back to their car. "Angee said Crazy Joe is out," Black told Bobby.

"Wonderful. He still talkin' 'bout killin' you?"

"Yup."

"That shit is crazy. He shoulda just waited for y'all to show up; not do the job by himself."

"They don't call him Crazy for nothin'," Black said.

As they got closer to his car, Bobby saw a Acura coming at them fast. When he saw the gun come out the window, he pushed Black to the ground and yelled, "Get down!"

Black and Bobby laid motionless as bullets rained over their heads. Once the car drove on, both men got up. "You all right?" Black asked.

"Yeah, you?"

"Yeah. I'm all right, but this shit is gettin' ridiculous. These kids gonna fuck around and make me start takin' this shit to them."

Chapter 23

It had been more than a week since Detectives Kirk and Richards paid a visit to Mike Black. And since then, nothing had happened to bring them any closer to closing the murders, and Richards was getting a little frustrated.

Both Stark and BB had all but disappeared from public life. The day after K Murder's death, BB scooped up all the drugs and money, picked up his girlfriend, and drove out to Long Island to hide out at her cousin's house in Wyandanch. Even his boyz didn't know where he was, and he liked it that way.

When BB didn't show up for K Murder's funeral, Stark began thinking that maybe he had the right idea. After the funeral, CeCe told him that Black had come to see her and said he wanted to meet with him to settle things. He immediately became suspicious. "What the fuck is you sayin'?"

"Black said to tell you that he ain't got no problem wit' you, and he wanna sit down wit' you to settle y'all's differences."

"What you mean Black came to you? How Black even know you?"

"He just walked up on me," CeCe said.

"When was this?"

"Last weekend, up on the avenue."

Stark had heard that some of Cash's boyz tried to hit Black on the avenue. Even if Black had told CeCe that he wanted to talk, them trying to kill him may have changed that. He suspected that if he went to that meeting, that he would be assassinated. "You tell Black that if he ain't got no problems wit' me, then I got none wit' him. I won't fuck wit' him and what he do, he don't fuck wit' me and mine. You tell him that, but I ain't goin' to no damn meeting. That ain't happenin'. You tell him I got nothin' to do wit' what Cash or K's boyz do," Stark said, and him and his boys walked away. The Commission was dead.

All CeCe could do was shake her head. Stark was practically shaking he was so scared of Black. All that, don't fuck with me and mine, shit he was talking must have been for his boys benefit, because she wasn't impressed.

Since that night, CeCe heard that Black had been to all the spots Stark hung out at night. "That's what you do when you got beef with somebody. You go lookin' for him, not hide like a bitch," CeCe told one of her girlfriends. "Mike Black is a real man. And I'm gonna get him."

"You're such a flirt. How can he resist you?" her girlfriend replied.

CeCe had been leaving word for Black with

anybody she could think of, but days had gone by and she still hadn't heard from him. She was starting to think that maybe she wasn't as irresistible as she thought she was.

When the detectives came to interview her for a second time and asked her if she knew Mike Black, CeCe started to ask them if they could get a message to him, but she didn't think they'd do it. So, when Richards and Kirk left her apartment, they still had nothing to go on.

"Any ideas?" Kirk asked.

"I'm fresh out," Richards confessed and slumped in his seat.

"What do you do when you've got nothin'?" Kirk asked and started the car.

"What?"

"You go make something happen."

"Where we goin'?"

"Taking a ride downtown."

"What for?"

"To talk to Agent Vinnelli," Kirk said as he drove. "See what he can tell us about the Commission."

"You think he might know something about these guys?"

"Not really, but you never know."

"I think you just like fuckin' with the guy," Richards said.

"I do." After his conversation with Black, Kirk knew that sooner or later he would hear that DeFrancisco was dead. That didn't bother him. In a way, he agreed that he had to die. *Justice?*

His concern was about Vinnelli.

Would Black really try to kill a DEA agent? Kirk didn't know.

Kirk had briefly entertained the idea of warning Vinnelli that Black was on to them and that he'd be coming. But he knew Vinnelli was dirty and suspected that he was the one who hired Kip Bartowski, the man who killed Shy.

Kirk had found a cigarette butt in the laundry room at Black's house. They were able to pull a partial print off of it. It came back that Bartowski was United States Army, Special Forces. He was reported killed in a training accident on October 27, 1998. His helicopter went down and the body was never recovered. "How could a dead man smoke a cigarette at a crime scene?" Kirk remembered asking Vinnelli during their investigation.

Even though he didn't say it, Kirk felt Black knew that Vinnelli was involved in the murder of his wife. So he had a decision to make.

Not my problem, Kirk decided. *If Vinnelli is murdered, it would be a federal matter. No one will ask me for my help. I been trying to get Black for murders I know for a fact that he committed and couldn't. Let's see if they can do any better. If they ask me, I'll tell them what I know, but they won't ask.* That he was sure of. But he did enjoy harassing Vinnelli, now more than ever.

While waiting for almost a half hour for Vinnelli, Richards occupied the time by flirting with the receptionist and pumping her for information about Vinnelli. He and Kirk had been there so many times over the last few months that the agent didn't bother coming to the lobby to greet them.

"Send them back. They know the way," Vinnelli

told the receptionist. When the detectives were seated before him, Vinnelli got right to it. "What can I do for you?" he asked, not bothering to hide his contempt.

"We're investigating the deaths of two suspected dealers," Kirk began with a look that showed his contempt. "We were hoping that you had something on them."

"Who we talkin' about?" Vinnelli asked.

Richards pulled out the crime scene photos. "A Steven Blake, goes by the name Cash Money. And the other one is Kevin Murdock," he said.

"Jesus," Vinnelli said, caught off guard by the bloody drive-by images. "What do they call him?"

"K Murder," Kirk spit out.

"Fitting, under the circumstances," Vinnelli laughed and Richards joined in. "I haven't heard of them, but give me a day or two to make some inquiries; you know, see if they come up on somebody else's radar and I'll get back to you."

"We would really appreciate that, Vinnelli," Richards said.

"Not a problem. Glad to help out. What's the deal with these clowns?"

Kirk was hoping he'd ask that question. "Those two and two others had formed what they called the Commission. They billed it as a buying co-op, but their real purpose was to protect themselves against Mike Black. I know you guys once considered him a person of interest, despite his lack of involvement in drugs."

"Don't tell me that fuck's involved?" Vinnelli asked.

"He's a suspect," Kirk said. "So any info you have to share may be helpful."

"I'll get right on it," Vinnelli promised.

"As always, we've taken up more than enough of your time," Kirk said and stood up. "Don't bother getting up, we know the way out."

Once the detectives were out of sight, Vinnelli got up and closed his door. He returned to his desk, picked up his phone, and dialed a number.

"Agent Masters," said the voice on the other line.

"Vinnelli. Detectives Kirk and Richards were just here."

"What did they want?" Masters asked.

"They're investigating the deaths of two drug dealers and they shared with me that Mike Black is a suspect."

"Really?"

"Kirk let that slip before he left." Vinnelli laughed a bit. "You heard anything about that?"

"I do need to make you aware of something, though."

"What's that?"

"Agent Harris has not been able to reacquire the other two subjects. If he can't resolve that situation soon, we may have to move up the timetable," Masters said.

"Keep me posted," Vinnelli said and hung up the phone.

Chapter 24

With a little help from Monika—a lot of help, actually—Jackie now had high-tech surveillance up and running on Mylo. After listening to the crude surveillance that Jackie had running, the first thing Monika wanted was to see the place. "All of it," she told Jackie when she came begging Monika to help her. "Gettin' up on his cell phone frequency is easy. I need to see the house."

"That's no problem," Jackie said. "Just come with me tonight."

"Don't you think that'll look a little suspicious? If I show up there and start wondering around?"

"Yeah, you're right. I didn't think of that," Jackie admitted.

"No, girlfriend, you're the one on the inside. You're the one who's gonna map the whole thing out, and you're the one who's gonna plant your devices. I'll be right back," Monika said and left Jackie alone in the living room.

While she waited, Jackie thought that whatever Monika had in mind wasn't helping her. She had already done her best work, and it was poor. *That's why I came to her in the first place*, Jackie thought. This was important to her. Black asked her to watch Mylo and she wanted to do a good job. She understood that it should turn in to better things for her. If Black trusted her, maybe he'd put her in a spot where she wouldn't have to hustle every night.

When Monika returned, she was wearing sunglasses, had a headset on, and was carrying a laptop. Jackie stood up.

"Where you goin'?" Monika said and sat down.

"I thought we were goin' somewhere." Jackie reclaimed her seat.

"Chill out a minute," Monika said, and opened her laptop. She handed Jackie an earpiece. "Put that in your ear and tell me if you can hear me." Jackie put the small device in her ear. "Can you hear me?"

"In my ear," Jackie replied.

Once Monika was set up, she handed the sunglasses to Jackie. "Put these on."

Jackie put the glasses on and Monika turned the laptop so she could see it. "Those are photosensitive sunglasses with a micro-miniature camera."

"Cool. It's just like I'm looking through sunglasses."

"What you see is recorded using a standard video recorder that is fed into a video transmitter in the lap. You go in wearin' those glasses and that earpiece. When I say *pan right*, you turn your head slowly to the right," Monika instructed and demonstrated how she wanted Jackie to do it. "When I say *pan left*, you turn your head slowly to the left. This way I can see the whole place and know where the best places are to set your cameras and microphones."

That night, Monika guided Jackie as she walked through the gambling house. The next night she told her where and how to set the devices. The only one that was difficult was the one in Mylo's office. Jackie came up with a reason to have to talk to Mylo alone in his office. Halfway through the conversation, Jackie said she wanted a drink. When Mylo went to get it, Jackie quickly did her work and was sitting pretty when he came back.

After a week of watching and listening to nothing even remotely important, both in the house and on his cell phone, Monika caught a break.

"Mylo."

"Who's this?" Mylo asked.

"You know who this is."

"What's up? Where you at?"

"Where I am ain't important. We need to talk, man. Shit has got real fucked-up. That nigga Black's been lookin' all over the city for me."

"Calm down, nigga, I got you. We can talk, just not over the phone. Where you at?" Mylo asked again.

"Don't worry about where I am. You just meet me at the Shrine Bar."

"I'll be there in an hour."

Monika had a feeling that if they were talking about Black, it might be something. She immediately called Jackie. "Fold and get out here," Monika said in Jackie's ear. She cursed and folded the king high straight she was working on and joined Monika in the car.

"What's up?" Jackie asked.

"We need to follow your boy," Monika said and explained what she heard. "He should be coming out that door right about now." Just as she spoke the words, Mylo came out of the house and walked quickly to his car. Monika closed the laptop and started the car. "Finally, a little action."

Mylo got in his car and headed downtown, with Monika trailing him. Since she knew where he was going and had a tracking device on his car, Monika was able to hang back so Mylo wouldn't notice them. On the way, Monika told Jackie where they were going.

The Shrine Bar restaurant was located in Harlem, on Seventh Avenue between 133rd and 134th Streets. It was a showcase for live music and boasted of having the best sound system in town. Mylo went inside and Monika waited a while and went in after him. By the time she got inside, Mylo was at the bar talking to a man she had never seen before. Since Monika was wearing her photosensitive glasses, Jackie was able to see what she was seeing. "I've never seen him before," Jackie confirmed.

The music was so loud that Monika knew even if she could get close enough to them, she wouldn't be able to hear what they were saying. And wouldn't be able to filter out all the background noise if she could plant a listening device. She was able to get pictures of the two of them talking and went back to the car.

The conversation lasted about fifteen minutes,

after which Mylo left the Shrine and walked back to his car. It wasn't too long before they picked up Mylo on his cell phone. A male voice answered the call on the second ring. "How long?"

"One hour," Mylo replied and ended the call.

The ladies followed Mylo back uptown to the Baychester Diner on Boston Road. Once again they waited as Mylo went inside. "Take pictures of everybody who goes in," Monika told Jackie.

"Where are you goin'?" Jackie asked.

"Inside," Monika said and got out.

Monika spotted Mylo sitting at a table in the back near the restrooms. She quickly grabbed her mouth and rushed up to the waitress. "Where's your restroom?"

When the waitress pointed toward the back, Monika walked quickly, still holding her mouth, more so to hide her face at this point. Mylo didn't look up when Monika passed his table. She brushed up against it and was able to place a listening device under the table.

Monika got back in the car with Jackie. "Are we live?" she asked.

"He just ordered coffee," Jackie told her and the two made themselves comfortable taking pictures and waited to see who Mylo was meeting.

Exactly one hour after Mylo made his call, a black Cadillac CTS pulled into the parking lot.

Chapter 25

Mylo sat in his booth at the Baychester Diner sipping his coffee. He looked at his watch and knew that he wouldn't have to wait too much longer. He had just left the Shrine Bar where he had met Bruce Stark, the so-called chairman of the Commission. Stark called him, frantically demanding that Mylo meet him to talk about Mike Black.

" 'Bout time you got here," Stark said when Mylo approached him at the bar.

"I'm here now, so what's the problem?" Mylo asked and marveled at how well his plan was going.

"I told you, fuckin' Black is the problem. That nigga is out to get me."

"What you expect, you sent somebody to kill him. What you think he was gonna do; throw you a party? Run out of town?"

"You the one that said he wasn't untouchable,

Mylo. After he killed Cash, you were the one who said he can be got just like any other nigga."

"Yeah, I did. And I meant it. I told you the best time to get him. I told you where the muthafucka would be. It ain't my fault that you fucked 'round and sent a nigga that couldn't get the job done. Now you come cryin' to me and say I fucked this up, now do something to help me."

"So what now?" Stark asked.

"What you mean, what now? You blew your shot to kill him. Now you got two choices," Mylo told him.

"What's that?"

"Make peace or get out of the city," Mylo advised, believing that Stark would choose to get out with his life.

"What?"

"You heard me, nigga. Music ain't that loud you can't hear me. Either you need to leave the city or try to make peace with him, 'cause that nigga ain't gonna stop. He will kill you."

"CeCe said he wanna sit down to work out our problems," Stark informed Mylo.

"CeCe? What the fuck she got to do with this?" Mylo demanded to know. Black meeting with Stark would ruin everything he had set in motion.

"She said he just walked up on her and told her that shit. Black and Bobby been in the street lookin' for me. Not Freeze, Black him-fuckin'-self."

"That's the last fuckin' thing you should do."

"But, you just said I could make peace with him. Now you sayin' I shouldn't?"

"Can't you see that shit? Do I have to tell you

every-fuckin'-thing?" Mylo asked and Stark didn't say anything. "Look, if you was to call for a meet, you could walk in there and say that it was all Cash and K and that you had nothing to do with it. But if he lookin' for you, then he know you was the one that sent that muthafucka to kill him."

"Right, right," Stark agreed.

"But if you meet him now, one, it will make you look like a weak nigga who wanna scream peace after they started shit. He won't respect you and sure as shit Black will kill you at that meeting."

"That's fucked-up, Mylo, you know that? For some shit that was your fuckin' idea, for you to stand there now and tell me some shit like that. I oughta shoot you my fuckin' self."

"But you won't," Mylo said and showed Stark the gun in his hand. "Where's BB?"

"His boys say he's ghost. Nigga took all the dope and money and gone."

Damn, Mylo thought. "Look, let me know where you gonna be and I'll see if I can't talk to Freeze, you know, like I said, tell him it was Cash and K."

"Now you talkin'. But you don't need to know where I'll be. I'll get in touch with you. You just get it done," Stark said and handed Mylo an envelope. "Earn your money. I ain't exactly sure that I can trust you. Far as you know, I'm at Foxwoods."

"Whatever, nigga. You ain't got to trust me." Mylo held up the envelope that Stark had just given him. "This all the trust I need from your ass," Mylo told Stark and left the Shrine Bar.

Stark was right not to trust Mylo, because Mylo had a plan. His plan was simple: organize what was left of Birdie's old crew, kill them off, and then take over their markets. It was a plan that he knew would work perfectly, but he knew he couldn't do it alone. He would need some help.

Just then, Mylo looked up and saw DEA Agent Masters come into the diner. Mylo and Agent Masters used to work together, cut a few corners together, and made a lot of money shaking down the very dealer they were assigned to investigate and bring to justice. This went on until Mylo was reassigned and began working undercover.

When Mylo determined that he couldn't carry out his plan alone, the person he turned to was Masters. When the two first talked about it, Masters didn't seem all that interested in Mylo's plan to take over the drug market, but a week later, Masters called and said he wanted to meet.

Mylo insisted that the meeting take place at a small bar in Stamford, Connecticut, where he could be sure he wouldn't be recognized meeting with the agent. When Masters arrived at the meeting, he wasn't alone. DEA Agent Pete Vinnelli was with him.

"Who's this?" Mylo asked as soon as he saw Vinnelli.

"You asked for my help, right? All you need to know is that he is part of the help you want," Masters said.

"I'm a friend of a friend of yours, Mylo. Or could I call you Clint?" Vinnelli asked.

"What friend?" Mylo needed to know.

"DeFrancisco," Vinnelli said simply.

At that point, Mylo knew exactly what the deal was, and he wasn't sure if it was a good thing or not. Before DeFrancisco went to jail, Mylo had begun working for him. When Mylo was arrested, his first thought was that somebody realized that he was out there without a handler and they were bringing him in. He began to worry when federal marshals took him to the airport and flew him to North Carolina and deposited him in some small-town jail. After three weeks in that cell, Mylo woke up one morning to find Agent DeFrancisco standing in front of him.

DeFrancisco told Mylo that he knew what he'd been doing and showed him a picture to prove it. At first, DeFrancisco gave Mylo a choice: "Turn over all the evidence to me or you'll be going to jail for a very long time." For Mylo, the choice was a no-brainer. DeFrancisco put him in touch with Birdie's partner, Albert. But then DeFrancisco went to jail and left Mylo making crazy money with no handler.

Now, Vinnelli's presence at this meeting meant that he would have to cut him in on the deal. Mylo barely trusted Masters, but at this point, he had no choice. He took a deep breath and laid out his plan for the agents. Masters had plenty of questions to ask Mylo about how this or that would work out, while Vinnelli remained quiet.

Once Mylo was done, Vinnelli finally spoke. "Okay, Clint, we'll help you, but you gotta do something for us."

"What's that?" Mylo asked.

"We'll provide the men to kill the dealers. But only if you convince this commission that Mike Black is the one responsible for the murders and that they go after Black in response to the murders. That and twenty-five percent." Vinnelli laughed that night. Naturally, Mylo agreed and the Commission murders began.

"What's up, Mylo?" Masters said as he sat down in the booth.

"Ain't nothin'," Mylo said as the waitress came to the table to refresh his coffee.

"What can I get you?" the waitress asked as she poured.

"Just a cup of coffee," Masters said. "Do you have any pie?"

"Best apple pie in the Big Apple."

"Well, we'll just have to see about that. Why don't you bring me a slice of pie, sweetie." Once the waitress was gone, Masters turned his attention to Mylo. "You hear anything from Stark or that other clown yet?"

"BB's in the wind, but he'll turn up. I just left Stark at the Shrine Bar. He wouldn't tell me where, but I think he's hidin' out somewhere in Harlem. Give me a couple of days and I'll have them both in place for you."

Masters leaned back and thought for a second or two. "We'll worry about them later. We're moving up the timetable."

"Why?"

"You ask too many questions, Mylo. What is going to happen now is that you are going to get Mike Black in place."

"Like I told you, he don't come into the city much, and when he does, he goes to Cynt's, picks up that same ho, and breaks to that hotel. But I doubt if he goes back there after what happened. You should have sent your own team."

"Don't worry, he'll meet my team soon enough. You just get him in place. I'll take care of the rest."

Mylo paused when the waitress returned with pie and coffee for Masters. Masters observed the look on Mylo's face and asked, "What?"

"Stark said that Black and Bobby Ray have been in the city looking for him."

"Ray always with him?"

"How the fuck should I know?" Mylo said angrily.

"Calm down."

"Fuck that shit. The deal was for you to kill all four of them, not just two—all fuckin' four. Now your smug ass wanna sit there and tell me we're moving up the timetable."

"Lower your voice," Masters cautioned and calmly ate his pie.

"Don't you think I know what's gonna happen when you get Black?"

"What's gonna happen, Mylo?"

"You're gonna leave killin' Stark and BB to me and you're still gonna want the cut we agreed on."

Masters smiled. "That's pretty much right. But you're forgetting one thing."

"What's that?"

"Black and Bobby Ray believe these clowns are the ones tryin' to kill him. When my team gets Black, what do you think your boy Freeze is gonna do?"

"Blow up the city."

"Right." Masters stood up and threw some money on the table. "Call me when you got him in play," he said and walked toward the door.

Meanwhile, out in the car, Monika and Jackie had heard and recorded each word. All Jackie could say was, "Wow."

"I know, that shit is deep," Monika agreed as she snapped a picture of Agent Masters leaving the diner. "You got to tell Black about this."

"I know," Jackie said and then she realized that she had no way of contacting Black. "He doesn't have a cell and I don't know Bobby's."

Monika snapped off a few shots of Masters getting in his Cadillac. "I could call Nick. He'll know how to get in touch with him," Monika said and pulled out her cell phone. She pressed Nick's speed dial number and the phone rang once before going to voice mail. "Shit! Since that nigga started fuckin' Wanda, he don't ever answer his phone."

"Nick is fuckin' Wanda?"

"Yup."

"Oooh, Nick," Jackie giggled.

"What now?" Monika asked.

"Take me to Cynt's. She'll know how to contact Black."

Chapter 26

Mike Black

It has been a long day and an even longer week, but I was havin' a ball. It was just like old times. Me and Bobby had been ridin', lookin' for this nigga Stark. He had gone underground and nobody had seen or heard from him or this other muthafucka I heard was down with him.

With nothin' else to go on, I decided to run down CeCe and see if she had given my message to Stark. She wasn't hard to find. CeCe had been leavin' messages for me with anybody with a pulse that she needed to talk to me, but wouldn't say what it was about. I guess she didn't want Cash's people thinkin' she was the one who set Cash up. The whole situation would be funny if it wasn't me these youngsters were trying to kill. I was glad that I had taken Michelle to stay with my mother. I couldn't be out here like this if I had to worry about her.

I rolled up on CeCe the same place I found her

the last time, on the dance floor, makin' that big, juicy ass she was carrying bounce. And just like last time, I stood where I knew she would see me, and once I got her attention, I pointed toward the bar.

CeCe smiled and nodded her head and I went to the bar to wait for her. I grabbed a seat at the bar and watched her dance. Me and Bobby were on our second shot of Rémy when she finally dragged herself off the dance floor. "You're a hard man to find," CeCe said and kissed me on the cheek.

"What was that for?"

"Just somethin' I been thinkin' 'bout doin' since the last time I saw you." CeCe leaned closer to me. "Only when I'm thinkin' 'bout kissin' you, it ain't on the cheek."

"I'll give you two some privacy," Bobby said and started to get up.

"No," I told him and he sat back down. CeCe was wearin' a tight black V-neck top that displayed an ample amount of cleavage and some jeans that looked like they were painted on her. She looked good, damn good, but I wasn't here for that, even though the more I looked at her, the more interested I was in her. But she didn't need to know that. All she needed to know is that I wanted Stark. "You talk to Stark yet?"

"Yeah, I talked to him at K's funeral," CeCe told me.

"You tell him what I said?"

"Yep. He said if you ain't got no problems wit' him, then he got none wit' you." Then CeCe smiled and I wondered why. "He said he won't fuck wit' you and what you do as long as you don't fuck wit' him and what he got goin'. He said he ain't got nothin' to do wit' what Cash or K's boyz do. But he ain't goin' to no damn meeting. That ain't happenin'."

That wasn't the answer I wanted to hear and I guess she knew that, and that's why she was smiling. She did tell me that Billy Banner was the fourth member of this so-called Commission. I knew his brother, Darryl, back in the day; he was a stand-up guy, as Angelo would say. The way I get it, Billy was nothing more than a place-holder. Darryl still ran the crew from his cell. I respected him, so I got a message to him about what was going on between me and his brother.

It took less than a day for word to come back to me that Darryl knew nothin' about his crew being part of any commission. The word was that they were lookin' for Billy 'cause he bounced with all the money and product.

The week wasn't a total loss. CeCe told me who it was that pulled the drive-by on me and Bobby. "They tryin' to make rep, tellin' anybody who'll listen."

And then CeCe told me where I could find them. "You sure about this?" I asked her.

"Yes, baby. I'm sure. I would never lie to you," CeCe said and pressed up against me. In my predator days, there was a rule that I used to live by: If a woman sets it out for me like she was doin', she would get fucked, whether I really wanted her or not. Those days, I didn't give a fuck; I woulda taken her outta there and fucked her in the first dark spot I could find. And then I'd go do what I had to do. That was then; this is now.

"They been braggin' 'bout how they almost got y'all," CeCe said.

"Like almost actually counted for something."

"And how funny it was to see y'all runnin' like scared bitches," CeCe continued.

At that point, I knew that CeCe was a dangerous woman. She knew exactly what buttons to push. She was the type of woman who could get a weak muthafucka to do anything she wanted. But I wasn't no weak muthafucka.

"So when you and me gonna get together?" she said as sexy as she could.

I stood up and so did Bobby. "When I'm done." Then I thought about it. "Come with me." I had no idea what they looked like, but I knew that as soon as me and Bobby walked in the place, that they would recognize us, nut the fuck up, and start blastin'. Takin' CeCe along would make things easy.

She smiled at me like I told her to come get some dick. "Yes, baby."

CeCe said that there were three of them and they hung out at a spot on 233rd street. I told her to go inside and tell them that Stark was outside waitin' for them. "Tell 'em he wants to get back to business with the Commission and he need 'em to step it up."

"What if they don't believe me?" CeCe asked.

"Tell 'em you been thinkin' 'bout it and you wanna fuck all three of 'em," Bobby said. "All that body you carryin', they'll follow you anywhere."

"At least somebody in here noticed," CeCe said and got out of the car, and I enjoyed watchin' her walk.

"You gonna fuck her?" Bobby asked once she was inside. " 'Cause if you ain't, I will."

"Free country, Bob. You can fuck her if you want her. I don't give a fuck. I didn't think she was your type."

"Why? She got a pussy, don't she?"

"True. But she ain't skinny as a rail and she definitely ain't flat-chested. Ain't that how you like them?"

"I'm tryin' to broaden myself; try new things. I'm gettin' older now and I like a little more cushion than I'm used to."

"I ain't mad at you."

We had been waitin' about a half an hour when I looked up and saw CeCe come out the lounge with three niggas trailin' close behind her. "Where the fuck is she goin'?" Bobby asked.

"How should I know?" When I saw her get in a car with them and pull off, we followed them.

"How you know we can trust her?"

"We don't," I said as we followed them down 233rd.

"I mean, she could be leadin' us into a trap."

"You wanna back off? Call Freeze or Nick?"

"Hell no. Trap or not, these bastards gonna die tonight."

We followed them to the Oasis Motel on Boston Road. "I guess she went with the orgy story," I said.

"Smart girl."

They all got out of the car and one of them went to get the room while the other two stayed by the car with CeCe. She saw where we had parked and was lookin' at me while they felt her up. The look on her face screamed, *What the fuck you waitin' for?*

I wanted them in a room, chillin', thinkin' about gettin' some pussy. I had something special in mind for them. Something that would send a message to Stark and any other nigga that was down with this commission, or who even had dreamt about comin' after me over this bullshit. I had to let 'em know that I wasn't somebody that they needed to be fuckin' with.

"You still ride with the sawed-off and a hunting knife in the trunk?" I asked.

"I never leave home without it," Bobby replied.

"Good," I said and put on my gloves.

"Ain't the shotgun gonna make too much noise?" Bobby asked.

"I'm not plannin' on shootin' it," I told Bobby, and put silencers on both of my guns. He was more than just my partner and my best friend; he was my brother.

Once they had their room key, we watched as they went inside the room. I could see CeCe lookin' back at us. I could only imagine what was goin' through her mind as the door closed behind them. "Let's go."

Bobby went and got the knife and the sawed-off out of the trunk, along with some plastic handcuffs and a roll of duct tape. When we got to the door, I could hear the music playin' and them yellin' for CeCe to take it off. "You ready?" I asked.

"Let's do it," Bobby replied and kicked the door open. When I rushed in, one of them reached for his gun. I shot him in the hand before he could get to it. "Anybody else wanna try that?" Bobby asked with the shotgun pointed at one of their heads.

Complete silence was the answer he got.

I looked at the three of them for the first time in a good light. None of them could be any older than twenty. "You muthafuckas know who I am?"

Complete silence was the answer I got.

"I'm the nigga that's gonna kill you tonight," I said and turned to CeCe. "You can go now, CeCe."

"CeCe, you fuckin' bitch! You set us up!" one said.

"I'm'a kill you!" the other said.

Me and Bobby laughed and so did CeCe. "No, nigga," CeCe said and got in his face. "Didn't you hear what the man said? You the one gonna die."

"I said leave," I reiterated.

"I'd rather stay," CeCe told me.

"I don't remember askin' you what you'd rather do."

"Please," she said in a voice that made me remember that she was dangerous.

"If you don't get the fuck outta here, I'll kill you too."

"Okay, okay," she said and started for the door.

"Before you go," Bobby said and handed her the duct tape. "Put tape over their mouths."

When she was done with that, I told her to put the plastic cuffs around their wrists and ankles. "Cuff those two to the chairs."

When she was done, CeCe came and stood next to me. "What now, baby?"

"Nothin'. Get out of here."

This time she didn't protest. "Yes, baby," CeCe said and walked toward the door. "Am I gonna see you again?"

"Yeah. Now get out."

As soon as CeCe slammed the door, I turned my attention to the three of them. "You muthafuckas gonna wish you were never born." I walked over to the one I shot. I pulled him up from the bed. I hit him a few times and then me and Bobby dragged him into the bathroom. We put him in the shower with his hands above the showerhead, then Bobby secured him to it with the plastic handcuffs. "You're gonna bleed to death," I said and ripped off his shirtsleeves. I could see the fear in his eyes. "Give me your knife, Bobby." I made two long cuts on each of his arms and a very small one on his neck.

I came out of the bathroom and looked at the other two. I got in one's face; he was scared too. "I'm gonna beat you to death," I said, and began hitting him in the face. When I stopped, Bobby took over.

Then I turned to the third. There was no fear in his eyes. When the other two were screaming about CeCe settin' 'em up and what they'd do about it, he was quiet.

"It was your idea to try me, wasn't it?"

He nodded his head slowly.

"You was gonna be the man that killed Mike Black."

He nodded his head slowly.

"I can respect that." And I could. I could see the position that it would put him in. If he killed me, he could go to Stark, who'd been hidin' from me, in a position of power.

"Too bad you missed and you gotta die for it," Bobby added and continued his work.

"I'm gonna kill you quick; break your neck. But not before you watch me kill your boys."

For the next hour or so, me and Bobby took turns beating our would-be executioners while his partner looked on. Every so often, I went into the bathroom to check on the bleeder. I came out and grabbed their leader. "Come on. I wanna show you something," I said and pushed him in the bathroom. He flinched and tried to look away, but I grabbed his face and made him look. "Look at him!"

By this time the bleeder was covered in blood and shaking. The leader had sat there calmly and watched his boy take a beatin', and didn't flinch or close his eyes not once, but this scared him.

"He's shakin' 'cause he's goin' into shock, he's startin' to get cold and he'll start losin' color." I pushed him out of the bathroom and he stumbled to the floor.

"Get up," I said and pulled him up and back into his chair so he could watch Bobby work. I watched Bobby and thought about us two old guys doin' shit we ain't done in years. It felt great. Then Bobby went old-school style on him.

Back in the day, Bobby's idea of torture was while he slapped the guy around, he'd tell jokes. Some of them were funny, but most of them weren't. If you laugh, you get slapped. If you don't, you get hit—hard. Only this guy got duct tape covering his mouth so he couldn't laugh. So Bobby was just whalin' away, tellin' your-mother jokes, and swingin'. "Your mother is so ugly that they had to hang a pork chop around her neck so the dog would play with her."

About two hours into it, Bobby got a call from Nick. "Bobby. Is Black with you?"

"He's right here. It's Nick," Bobby said and handed me the phone.

"What's up, Nick?"

"I just got a call from Monika. She wouldn't say what it was about, but she said Jackie needs to talk to you."

"And she didn't say what, huh?" I asked, wondering what Jackie could possibly want.

"Nope, but Monika wouldn't call if it wasn't important."

"Okay, call her back and tell them to meet me at Cynt's," I said and pressed end. When I handed Bobby back his phone, he was laughing. I didn't tell him that I made Mystique stop working there, and I didn't feel like goin' into it. "Let's wrap this up," I said and went in the bathroom and shot the bleeder twice in the head. When I came out, Bobby was doing the same to the other.

I walked up behind the leader. I promised to break his neck. I picked up the sawed-off shotgun by the butt, and swung it as hard as I could to the back of his neck. I don't know if it actually broke his neck and I really doubt that it did, but his neck and head did jerk forward. I walked around in front of him, shot him twice in the head, and followed Bobby out the door.

Chapter 27

Jackie and Monika sat at Cynt's and waited patiently for Black to get there, or at least Monika did. Jackie was nervous and couldn't sit still for very long. She'd be all right for a while, but then she'd bounce up and walk around, just in case he was there and she just couldn't see him while she was sitting down.

"I wish you'd stop doin' that," Monika said when Jackie came back and sat down. To her, waiting to report was nothing new and she seemed content sipping her drink and people watching.

"I can't help it," Jackie said and picked up her watered-down drink.

"I understand, but finish your drink and relax. He'll get here when he gets here. You like pussy, don't you?" Monika asked. "Well, there's plenty in here to look at."

"I noticed you gettin' your eyes full, Ms. I'm strictly-dickly," Jackie came back.

"How could you not? It's very compelling to watch. The atmosphere, energy of the dancers, the raw sexuality of it all, you know what I'm sayin'? I mean, just the look on some of these guys' faces is priceless."

"I know. It's like they've never seen a naked woman before. I never have understood that one," Jackie said as she stood up again and noticed that Black and Bobby had come in.

Since Mylo had mentioned Cynt's so prominently in his conversation with the man he'd met earlier in the evening, Jackie was apprehensive about them meeting Black there. She wanted to tell Monika to call Nick back and insist that they should meet somewhere else, but she didn't want to seem like she was overreacting.

As soon as he saw her, Black made eye contact with Jackie. He was on his way to her when Cynt cut him off.

As soon as Black saw Cynt storming toward him, he knew what she wanted. He had meant to talk to her about telling Mystique that he didn't want her dancing there, but he just hadn't gotten around to it. "We need to talk, Mr. Black."

"Yes we do, Cynt," Black said. "How's business tonight?"

"Good night," Cynt replied. "Good night. But it would be better if Mystique hadn't quit on me. And when I asked her why, she says I should ask you."

By this time, Bobby was beside himself with laughter. "Mystique quit? What you know about that?"

Black ran his hand over his face. "I told her she didn't work here any more."

"Oh," was the only answer Cynt could manage.

"I was gonna talk to you about it, but I been busy."

"If there was some problem with her, I'm sure we can work it out," Cynt said, believing that he had fired her. "Mystique is one of my best earners, Black, so—"

"Cynt, there's no problem. I just don't want her workin' here," Black tried to explain without having to go into any detail.

"He's claimin' her, Cynt," Bobby said.

"Oh, that's different. Now it's business," was her comment.

"I know, Cynt. I'll compensate you for the loss of income. Think of a price, just don't get ridiculous," Black said as the room exploded in applause. Frank Sparrow, the middleweight champion of the world, had just came in Cynt's and was immediately mobbed by both dancers and fight fans.

"I guess we'll talk about this later, Black. Let me go make the champ spend some money."

"Oh, hell no, Cynt," Bobby said and grabbed Cynt by her arm. "Don't do that. The fight is tomorrow night, so he don't need to be playin' poker all night or leave here with two or three hoes. I got money ridin' on him."

"Okay," Cynt said and snatched her arm back. "And don't be grabbin' me. I ain't one of these young girls you be all over in here."

"Don't hate, Cynt, you can get some too," Bobby said, remembering that Cynt used to give good head back in the day.

"Whatever, Bobby," Cynt said and walked away.

Bobby turned to Black. "Why didn't you tell me you were claimin' amazon Shy?"

" 'Cause I didn't want to hear your mouth."

"You did right. If you gonna keep fuckin' her."

"And I am."

"It didn't look right to have what everyone considers your woman shakin' her ass for every nigga that rolls through."

"I'm glad you approve," Black said and Jackie caught his eye once again. "Come on. Let's go see what Jackie's talkin' 'bout."

Jackie stood up when she saw Black coming, until she heard, "Black! Yo Black!" Frank Sparrow yelled as he and his entourage made their way toward Black. He smiled at Jackie and she sat down again to wait her turn.

"What's up, champ?" Bobby said.

"Mr. Ray, Mr. Black," Sparrow said, showing respect.

"You got it, champ," Black said.

"Ready for tomorrow?" Bobby said.

Sparrow raised his right fist. "He ain't ready for this. I got too much speed and too much power for him. He's goin' down," he said and feinted his right to Bobby's jaw.

"Watch out now. Niggas have died for less shit than that," Bobby laughed and motioned for his gun.

While Bobby talked shit with Sparrow's entourage, the champ looked at Black. "What's the matter, Frank?" Black asked.

"I'm cool, Black. It's all good," he said and quickly leaned toward Black. "Everythin's set for tomorrow."

"What?"

"It's all set."

"What are you talkin' about?"

Sparrow took a step closer and whispered in Black's ear, "Everything is set for me to go down."

Black leaned back with his eyes opened wide in shock of what the champ had just told him. Black grabbed Sparrow by the arm. "We need to talk," Black said and turned to Sparrow's handlers. "I need to talk to the champ for a second."

"No problem, Black," one handler said.

"Bobby, you're with me," Black said and led Sparrow up the stairs to Cynt's office. Once they were behind closed doors, Black asked, "What the fuck are you talkin' 'bout?"

"Everything is all set for me to do that for you."

"Do what for me?"

"You know, take a dive in the first."

"What the fuck is you talkin' 'bout, Frank?" Bobby asked.

"You need to tell me everything, Frank," Black said.

"You don't know nothing about this?" Frank was puzzled.

"I don't know anything about you takin' no dive."

"I knew I shouldn't trust that muthafucka; that's why I made sure I came by here. You know, to make sure that's what you still wanted."

"What muthafucka?" Black demanded to know.

"Mylo."

"Mylo? Who the fuck is Mylo?" Bobby asked.

"Y'all don't even know this nigga?" Sparrow questioned.

"I know him," Black said and looked at Bobby. "He runs the game for us."

"Our game?" Bobby asked.

"Our game," Black said definitely. "So what did he say I wanted you to do?"

"Since bettin' been real strong and a lot of action on what round, he said since everybody knows I'm a slow starter that no one will think twice about me gettin' caught with a clean shot early."

"You good with that?" Black asked.

"He said you was counting on me. Mylo said that since they insisted on a rematch clause in the contract, that I'd get the rematch and I'd just kick his ass in the second fight."

"Why didn't we think of that?" Bobby asked.

" 'Cause it ain't right, that's why. You're the middleweight champion of the world, the undefeated champ at that. This is your legacy, Frank. You have a chance to be great. I'm talkin' Marvelous Marvin Hagler, Carlos Monzón, Bernard Hopkins kind of great."

"Sugar Ray Robinson?"

"Let's not get carried away," Black said and Bobby nodded in agreement.

"They don't make fighters like that no more," Bobby said.

"But even that's possible, Frank. But I don't think you gonna hang around long enough to win one hundred and seventy-five fights," Black said and put his arm around the champ. "All I'm sayin' is that I would never ask you to do no shit like that. Not for money."

"Yeah," Bobby said. "You unify them belts, defend your title twenty-one times, and retire undefeated as champion."

"That's what I'm talkin'," Sparrow said, nodding his head.

"One more thing," Black said. "When I want you to do some shit like that, and that day may never come, you'll hear it from me. And Frank, try warmin' up before the fight. No weaknesses."

"Got ya," Sparrow said and started for the door.

"Hey, Frank," Bobby called to him before he left the office. "He goes down in the first."

"Bet on it," Sparrow said.

"I did," Bobby said as Sparrow raised a fist and closed the door behind him.

"Let's see what Jackie wants," Black said when Sparrow left the room. Bobby opened the door and Black followed him out.

When Black and Bobby got with Jackie, she insisted that they had to talk in private. "I need for you to listen to something," Jackie said and pointed at the laptop that Monika was carrying.

"What's it about?" Black asked.

"Mylo," Jackie answered.

"Mylo? Why don't I know this nigga?" Bobby said.

"What about Mylo?" Black questioned.

"You remember you told me to watch Mylo 'cause you didn't trust him? Well, you were right not to trust him. This nigga is grimey for real."

It wasn't long before the four were in Cynt's office. Monika set up the laptop and played back the conversation that she and Jackie recorded earlier in the evening. The recording was a little staticky, and there was a lot of background noises, but they were able to hear what they needed to hear.

> *You hear anything from Stark or that other clown yet?*
>
> *BB's in the wind, but he'll turn up. I just left Stark at the Shrine Bar.*

"Who's that he's talkin' to?" Black asked.

"This is him," Monika replied and showed Black a picture of Agent Masters and the car he drove up in.

> *. . . We're moving up the timetable.*
>
> *Why?*
>
> *You ask too many questions, Mylo. What is going to happen now is that you are going to get Mike Black in place.*
>
> *Like I told you, he don't come into the city much, and when he does, he goes to Cynt's, picks up that same ho, and breaks to that hotel.*

"He set up the hit at the hotel," Bobby said.

"Seems that way," Black agreed.

"Shhh. This part is important," Jackie said and both Black and Bobby looked at her. The four of them sat and listened to the rest of the conversation. Once the recording was finished, Black sat quietly and looked at the rest of the images that Monika had snapped. Black looked at Jackie. "I'm impressed," he said.

Jackie smiled. "Are you really?"

"Really. You did good."

"Well, Monika did all the hard work," Jackie said modestly.

"That's not true, Black. I just helped her out," Monika corrected. "It was Jackie's plan. She planted all of the devices."

"Don't matter who gets the credit," Bobby finally said. "This answers a lot of questions. It's been these two assholes pullin' the strings. Had all of us dancin' to their beat. We need to find out who this other guy is."

"Question is, what timetable are they moving up?"

"Killin' you."

"Since they're onto this place, it's a good bet that they know you're here," Monika said.

"That means they'll be coming." Jackie finally said what she had been feeling all along. She checked her gun and so did Monika.

"Let 'em come," Bobby said and started walking toward the safe in the office. Cynt kept a small arsenal in that safe, as well as two other places in the club.

"Slow down, everybody," Black said with his hands in the air. "If they know about this place, then they gotta know this ain't the place to come at us."

Bobby started laughing a little. "You're right. We could fight a small army off with the shit we got here."

"Black's right," Monika said. "They wouldn't try it here. Semipublic place; too many variables they couldn't control, too much could go wrong," she added.

"That's right," Black said and stood in front of Monika. "This is your type of shit. How would they do it?"

"Shit, there are hundreds of ways they could come at you. But I can tell you this, they already know how and they know where they're gonna come at you. They are either gonna lead you there, or just wait for you to show up.

Chapter 28

After Black and Bobby left Cynt's, they went straight to Bobby's house and had a few of their men meet them there. Bobby quickly got his family out of bed and ready to leave the house. He didn't believe that they were in any real danger, but Bobby felt safer with them out of the house. Once he was satisfied that his family was safe at a hotel with men to watch over them, he drove back to the city with Black.

"Where you wanna go now?" Bobby asked as they drove across the Tappan Zee Bridge.

"Take me by Maria's apartment," Black answered, referring to Mystique by her government name for the first time.

"Who?"

Black looked at Bobby. "Amazon Shy."

"I'm'a stop callin' her that. Now that you claimin' her and shit."

"Call her whatever you want, just take me by

there. Since they know about her too, I want to make sure she's safe."

"I'll put a couple of our people on her," Bobby said.

"No," Black said definitely. "She'll be all right with me."

"I'm sure she will, but I'm still gonna put somebody on her and you too."

"No."

"Look Mike, I don't give a fuck what you say, you gonna have somebody on you."

"I got you."

"Yeah, but I'm gonna go to sleep sometime. Somebody's gonna be watchin' our back. And besides, you ain't plannin' on takin' her to Carolina with us, are you?"

"Hell no."

"Then she needs somebody on her until you get back," Bobby said as he drove.

"I guess you're right," Black admitted reluctantly.

"Of course I am. Ain't no harm in havin' a few bodies around until this blows over, right?"

But Black didn't answer him. He stared out the window and thought about Mylo. They had a traitor in their house, somebody that Freeze brought to him. Could Freeze have misjudged Mylo, or was he involved? There was no way he could be sure, but he knew he'd find out.

It had been a long time since somebody had betrayed him. His name was Gary Banks; he used to run one of their gambling houses until he got caught selling drugs. Back then, everybody that worked for Black made a pledge not to sell drugs.

After what he consider a fair trial in front of his peers, Black tortured and then executed Banks that night while everyone in the room looked on. Some people started to leave, but Black stopped them. He wanted to be sure that everyone there saw what was happening. Banks was gonna die that night and Black wanted to be sure all of them knew why. Black wondered would he give Mylo a chance to defend himself or would he just kill him.

Bobby looked at Black, waiting for him to say something about having a few bodies around. When he didn't answer, Bobby said it again. "Ain't no harm in havin' a few bodies around, right?"

"Huh?"

"I said, ain't no harm in havin' a few bodies around until this blows over."

"You're right."

"What zone you in?"

"Thinkin' 'bout this nigga Mylo and wonderin' 'bout Freeze."

"I wasn't gonna say anything, but I know you got to be thinkin' the same thing I am. Is Freeze involved in this thing? I mean, where this nigga come from that all of the sudden that Freeze got him runnin' our game? And how come nobody bothered to tell me 'bout him?"

"Freeze said that Jap meet him in jail. Jap used him on a couple things, and turned him on to Freeze."

"That's it?" Bobby asked, thinking that that damn sure wasn't good enough.

"All I can tell you is that Cassandra didn't like

him. That shoulda told me something. He was the one that told Freeze where Birdie and Albert were hidin' out."

"Anybody ask him how he knew where they were?"

"What?" Black asked.

"Did anybody ask him how he knew just where to find them?"

"I never thought about that."

"I been tellin' you for years, I look at shit a little differently than other people. And why should you have thought about that? You were in jail while they were out chasin' the wild goose. By the time you got out, they were dead and you moved on to the real killers."

"You're right," Black said, thinking back to those days.

"But think about that shit now. This fuckin' commission, all them niggas used to work for Birdie. Knowing that he's got some influence over them—" Bobby started.

"That's how he knew where to find Birdie and Albert. He was down with them," Black said.

"So we know he a snitch."

"I hate fuckin' snitches."

"But Freeze depends on them," Bobby pointed out. "He's made his rep on knowin' or being able to find out information. Information that you've relied on for years and you didn't give a fuck where it came from."

"What are you sayin', Bob?"

"Muthafuckas been snitchin' for Freeze for years, you can't hold that against him now, that's all I'm sayin'."

"Okay, but do you think Freeze knew about Mylo fixin' the fight or tryin' to kill me?"

"I don't think so. Maybe it is just bad judgement for him to trust Mylo, but Freeze is too loyal to you for him to be a part of that."

"I hope you're right. I don't even wanna think about that," Black said and looked out the window. The thought of Freeze betraying him was much more than he wanted to deal with right then. He didn't want to believe it, but there was no way that he could ignore the possibility. Freeze was like a brother, even a son to him. *There is no way.*

When they got back to the city, Black picked up Mystique and took her to the Marriott on Fortieth Street, where Bobby had two men waiting. She stayed awake and watched over Black while he slept for a couple of hours, before him and Bobby headed to North Carolina to settle a debt.

Chapter 29

After rotting for more time than he thought was possible in the federal prison camp in Atlanta, the day had finally come for him to get out of there. Former DEA Agent Kenneth DeFrancisco wasn't getting out of jail altogether, though. He still had thirteen more years on the fifteen-year sentence he was serving for his involvement with drug trafficking that, had it been successful, would've had Mike Black in there instead of him. Two days after he was taken into custody, the government confiscated all of his assets. His sprawling home, the condo on the North Carolina coast, his prized cars, motorcycles, even the cash he had neatly stashed in offshore accounts. The most important thing he lost was his wife.

He thought back to the last time he spoke to his wife, Jane. "They're putting me out?" she had cried that day. She had barricaded herself in the bedroom while IRS agents went through everything they owned. They hadn't paid taxes on millions of dollars. "Where am I supposed to go? What about the kids? You need to fix this! You need to fix this, now!" That last conversation with his wife woke him up every night and reminded him just how much he hated Mike Black.

Even that didn't matter that morning. For DeFrancisco, 6:00 AM couldn't come fast enough. He was up and dressed before five that morning and sat patiently waiting for something that he was beginning to think would never come. He was excited, because this particular morning, DeFrancisco was being transferred to another institution.

"And it's about damn time that arrogant prick Marshall got off his ass and did something for me," DeFrancisco said as he got up from his bed and began pacing back and forth in his cell.

Even though he was talkin' shit about it, he was at first surprised and then thankful the week before when the guard told him that he had a phone call.

"Somebody callin' me?" he asked. He very rarely got any phone calls, and the entire time he'd been there, only one visitor. As he got up and waited for the cell door to open, DeFrancisco thought that it could only be his old friend and partner, Pete Vinnelli, on the line for him. It was Vinnelli, dressed in biker gear and posing as DeFrancisco's lawyer, who was his lone visitor. *It couldn't be anybody else,* DeFrancisco thought as he was escorted off the cell block. When he got to the phone he was surprised when a female voice introduced herself after he said, "hello."

"Is this Kenneth DeFrancisco?" the perky-sounding female asked.

"Yes, this is," DeFrancisco responded curiously. He was sure that it was Vinnelli calling.

"My name is Danielle Summer. I am the personal assistant to Senator Martin Marshall. How are you today, Mr. DeFrancisco?"

"I'm fine," DeFrancisco said excitedly. The words *Martin Marshall* were more than enough to cause that reaction. He had been reaching out to Marshall through Vinnelli and writing him letters since the day he got to that shit hole to do something for him. DeFrancisco felt like Marshall owed him that for not snitching on him about his involvement with Diego Estabon in the very case he was doing time for.

"Senator Marshall sends his regards and best wishes to you, and his sincere apology for not being able to speak with you personally. Senator Marshall wants you to know that he has received all of your correspondence regarding a transfer to an institution in your home state due to the hardship it places on your minor children for visitation."

"That's refreshing to know," DeFrancisco said, encouraged by the direction the conversation was going.

"The senator wanted me to express that while he is understanding and very sympathetic to your situation," Danielle Summer explained, "he strongly encourages you to continue to go through the established channels to secure a transfer. The senator is confident that once your case is reviewed, that you will have no problem having your request approved. However, once you have exhausted all other remedies at your disposal without success, please, by all means, do not hesitate to write the senator again."

"You are sayin' that he won't help me? Is that what you called to say?" DeFrancisco asked angrily.

"Not at all, sir. What I said was, the senator is confident that once your case is reviewed, that you will have no problem having your request approved. That, sir, is what I said. Do you understand what I'm saying now?"

"Yeah, I understand," said a dejected DeFrancisco.

"Then you have a good day, sir." And with that, Danielle Summer ended the call.

On the way back to his cell, DeFrancisco felt like he had just had his insides kicked out. Not only wouldn't Marshall help him, he had the nerve to have some bitch call and tell him that he wasn't gonna do shit for him. His mood had lasted for a couple of days when he was once again escorted from his cell. This time he was taken to the administration area where he was informed that he was to be transferred to another federal prison camp.

"That is the very best news you could have possibly given me," DeFrancisco said. "Thank you, thank you very much."

On the way back to his cell, this time DeFrancisco thought back to his conversation with Marshall's assistant. *The senator is confident that once your case is reviewed, that you will have no problem having your request approved.* Now the call made sense to him. That was Marshall's way of telling him that he had gotten it done for him.

Now DeFrancisco took back almost every bad thing that he had ever said about Marshall. "Except for arrogant prick, 'cause that son of a bitch is one *arrogant prick,*" DeFrancisco said as he waited.

After DeFrancisco was processed, he was taken to Hartsfield-Jackson Airport, which was located just outside Atlanta, and flown to Raleigh, where he would serve the remainder of his time at a minimum-security facility housing male offenders, located in Goldsboro, North Carolina.

Once they got off of their flight, DeFrancisco and the officer made the seventy-two-mile drive to the federal prison camp located on Seymour Johnson Air Force Base, east of the city limits of Goldsboro. When they got off of I-40 East and got on US-70 East, the officer noticed a car coming up behind them, and it was closing in fast.

Thinking that the car was just another speeding motorist, the officer flipped on his lights to slow them down, but the car kept coming. Before he could react, the speeding car slammed into the back of his cruiser.

"What the fuck!" the officer said as he tried to regain control of his vehicle.

DeFrancisco bounced around in the backseat. "What the hell is goin' on?" he yelled.

"Some crazy son of a bitch just ran into the back of us!" he yelled as the car slammed into them again. The officer sped up and tried to get away. As he began to pull away, he reached for his radio, but was startled when he heard a loud noise. "They shot out our tire. Hold on!" he shouted to DeFrancisco. The officer grabbed the radio, but it fell out of his hand when the car slammed into the back of the cruiser again. This time the car stayed on them and rode them off the road.

Before the officer could regain his composure, two armed men wearing masks were on either side of the car. One quickly opened the driver-side door and dragged the officer out of the cruiser, while the other pulled out DeFrancisco. The shaken officer was led away from the car at gunpoint by one of the masked men and handcuffed to a nearby tree, while DeFrancisco was taken to their car by the other. "Who the hell are you?" DeFrancisco yelled as he struggled.

"I'm your executioner," the masked man said and hit the former agent with the butt of his gun, knocking him out cold.

When DeFrancisco came to and looked around, he was in what appeared to be an abandoned house. Once he began to move he could hear voices. "He's wakin' up, Mike."

"It's 'bout time. I didn't think I hit him that hard."

As DeFrancisco's eyes began to focus, he saw two black men coming toward him. One of the men immediately hit him in the face. "Who the fuck are you?" DeFrancisco yelled.

"You don't know who I am? After all the shit you did to me, you don't know who I am."

"No, I don't know who you niggas are or what you want, but I'm tellin' you—" DeFrancisco started, but his words were met with a fist in his face.

"It don't even matter if you know who I am. I just wanna ask you one question."

DeFrancisco spit blood from his mouth. "What?"

"Why did you kill my wife?"

DeFrancisco dropped his head, but quickly looked up at the man who stood before him. "Mike Black?"

"You see, he does know you, Mike," Bobby said.

"I cannot help but be touched," Black said and hit DeFrancisco again. "Why'd you do it?"

He hit DeFrancisco again. He spit blood again and began to laugh.

"What's so funny?" Bobby asked.

"He knows he's gonna die today," Black said and held his gun to DeFrancisco's head.

"It's a good day to die," Bobby said.

Black got in DeFrancisco's face. "Why'd you do it; why'd you have my wife killed?"

"I was married once," DeFrancisco said and laughed a little. "Married to a good woman. Sure, she was a little high-strung, but she was a good woman." DeFrancisco thought back to that last conversation he had with his wife. *Hold on a minute, Kenny. I know how to fix this.* Then DeFrancisco heard a noise, followed by more banging on the door. Then he heard a single shot. The IRS agents found Jane's body lying across their California king-sized bed. "She took her own life one day; took her own life because I couldn't be there for her. Since you want answers, you wanna know why I couldn't be there for her?" DeFrancisco asked, but didn't wait for an answer. "It was 'cause of you. 'Cause I was in jail where you should have been. It coulda been you rotting in that shit hole, not me. You!" DeFrancisco shouted. "My wife is dead because of this shit, so your wife had to die too."

Black hit DeFrancisco again. "That's it? That's why you killed my wife?" Black hit him again. "I never even heard of you; how the fuck you blame me for you being in jail? You should be blamin' your partner, Diego Estabon, for coming up with such a stupid idea."

"Easy to blame a dead man," Bobby joked.

Black looked at Bobby, but he didn't seem to be amused. He turned back to DeFrancisco. "You know I've dreamed about this day. Dreamed about how I was gonna kill you. I was gonna torture you, you know; just beat you and torture you for a day maybe, before I killed you." Black took a step back. He thought about his life with and without Cassandra. Black closed his eyes and could see her lying on the kitchen floor. Her face, beaten, bruised, and bloody. And what about Michelle? Forced to grow up without her mother. "But now I'm thinkin' I should just kill you," he said and raised his gun to DeFrancisco's head.

"Fuck you!" DeFrancisco yelled.

"No. Fuck you," Black said and fired two shots to his head. The impact of the shots were enough to knock DeFrancisco out of his chair. Bobby walked over and picked up two gas cans and handed one to Black. He poured gas over DeFrancisco's body, and then they poured gas around the abandoned house. Once the gas cans were empty, Black and Bobby walked out of the house. Black turned around and removed a book of matches from his pocket. He lit the book on fire and threw it into the house.

It didn't take long for the house to burst into flames; engulfing everything around it, including the car that they had stolen to kidnap the former agent. Black and Bobby stood off in the distance and watched until the car's gas tank caught fire and exploded. "You ready?" Bobby asked.

"Yeah, let's go," Black said and got in Bobby's car. "We got a fight to catch."

Chapter 30

It was ten o'clock on Friday night and the crowd was gathering at Madison Square Garden for the middleweight title fight between champion Frank Sparrow and the number-one contender, Irish Stevie Dudgeon.

Mike Black stretched out on the bed watching prefight coverage and waited for Mystique to get dressed. He had been dressed and ready to go for the last twenty minutes, but he didn't mind watching Mystique wander around their suite. Watching her stand in front of the mirror meticulously applying her makeup, made Black think about Cassandra. It never took her long to get ready, even though it always looked like she'd spent hours on her appearance.

"I'll be ready in a minute; I promise," Mystique said and picked up the dress that was laid out on the bed next to Black: a Donna Karan wrap-tie black dress, made from imported Italian fabric with a plunging V-neck, and long sleeves that tied at the center front.

"I'm not rushin' you."

"It's just that I wanna look nice for you."

"You look delicious right now," Black said and got off the bed.

"You know what I mean. This is kind of our first date and—you know—I just want to look nice for you, that's all."

Black started to say something about the whole first-date thing, but thought better of it.

Once Mystique had the dress on, she stood in front of him. "How do I look?"

"Like I should take it off of you, slowly," Black said.

"I'm ready if you are, but you'll miss your fight. You don't know the meaning of a quickie."

"Neither do you."

"I know." Mystique smiled. There was something she'd been wanting to ask him and this was as good a time as any. "You mind if I ask you a question?"

"Go ahead, ask me what you wanna know."

Mystique took a deep breath. "I know you said you didn't want me dancin' at Cynt's no more. I was just wondering what that meant for us?"

"What do you mean?" Black answered a question with a question, even though he hated it when people did it to him. He knew what she wanted to know, but wasn't in any mood to talk about it.

"What I'm askin' is, when you first asked me to stop dancin' was it 'cause of what you got goin' on, 'cause you were scared something might happen to me." Mystique took a step closer. "Or was it because of us?"

Black looked at Mystique in that tight-fitting black dress and that plunging neckline that showed off her abundant cleavage and thought about saying, *Can't we talk about this after the fight?* This was a conversation that he didn't feel like having. The same conversation he thought he was avoiding by not commenting on the whole first-date thing.

Black paused for a minute and thought about how he was going to answer her. There is no nice way to say, *It's bad for my rep for you to be dancin' there and I'm fuckin' you.* But was that all there was to it or was he really starting to feel something for her? He wasn't sure.

Then she let him off the hook. "I'm not askin' you for any kind of commitment or anything like that. I know you are nowhere near ready for anything like that." Then she thought about it. "Are you?"

"No," Black said quickly.

"And that's cool, really, it is. I just wanna know where I stand."

"You're good," Black said simply. "And not just because of my shit."

Mystique threw her arms around him like he had just confessed his love for her.

"Can we go see the fight now?"

"Sure we can, baby," Mystique said and took one last look at herself in the mirror. She grabbed her clutch bag and they were finally out the door.

After stopping in the dressing room to say hello to the champ, Black and Mystique made it to their seats just as the preliminary fight got started. It turned out to be a good fight. Being a real fan of the sweet science, Black loved every minute of it. Mystique sat next him, happy to be there with him, but hoping that the night would be over soon so they could go.

Once the preliminary bouts were over, more people began filing into the arena. Black sat looking around for Freeze and Mylo. He had called Freeze earlier in the day to make sure that both he and Mylo were coming to the fight. Black felt bad not telling Freeze exactly what was going on; he hated the fact that after all these years and all they'd been through together, that he wasn't sure that he could trust Freeze.

Mystique leaned in close to Black. "Why is that woman staring at you?"

"What woman?" Black asked and scanned the area with his eyes. They stopped on CeCe.

"Yeah, that one."

"Excuse me a minute, Maria," Black said and got up. "I'll be right back," he said and left Mystique sitting there with her eyes and mouth opened wide. She wasn't quite sure whether she was more upset that he left her to talk to another woman, or surprised that he called her Maria.

Black made his way through the crowd until he made it to CeCe. "Hello, Mr. Black."

"How you doin', CeCe?"

"Much better now that I've seen you. You look nice in a suit. You should wear them all the time. Not all men can carry a fine tailored suit, but you wear it well."

"You look nice too," Black said and got his eyes full looking at CeCe in that dress she was wearing the hell out of. It was a Just Cavalli cornucopia-print gown, with metallic gold spaghetti straps, and a flared mermaid hem.

"I'm glad you like it. I like doin' stuff that makes you happy."

"I'm surprised to see you here. You a fight fan?"

"Big-time fan. I love boxing," she said and leaned forward to emphasize her point when she said it. Black watched her lips when she talked, the way her words seemed to glide over them. "I got these tickets for Cash. Next week would have been his birthday. I was gonna surprise him with the tickets."

"No point lettin' them go to waste, especially since you love boxing. But what about that dress? Were you gonna surprise him with that too?"

"Not at all, baby. I got this dress yesterday. See, I knew *you* were gonna be here tonight and I wanted to look nice for you."

"So you got that dress for me?"

"Just for you, baby. And I am so glad you like it," CeCe said and took a step closer to him.

"I want you to do something for me."

"You know I will. Just tell me what you need me to do, baby."

"I need you to get in touch with Stark. I want you to tell him again that we don't have no problems. You tell him that Mylo was our problem."

"Mylo? Who is Mylo?"

"He'll know who he is. You tell him that it was Mylo playin' us against each other. But then you tell him that he ain't gotta worry 'bout him no more."

"Why is that?"

"You ask too many questions."

"What's the matter, don't like a thinking woman?"

"I love a thinkin' woman," Black had to admit.

"So why he ain't gotta worry about him no more? Just in case he asks," CeCe said. She was flirting with every word she said.

" 'Cause by the time you talk to him, Mylo will be dead."

"I understand," she said, as she smiled a very sexual smile. Like the fact that Black planned on killing Mylo turned her on. "So," CeCe said and peeked around Black. "Is that your woman you sittin' wit'?"

"Now you worried 'bout the wrong thing. You just do what I need you to do for me," Black said and started to walk away from CeCe. "And I'll see you around."

"That you can count on," CeCe said definitely and watched Black until he reclaimed his seat next to Mystique.

"Who was that?" Mystique asked before he sat down.

"Just somebody I needed to carry a message for me. Why?"

" 'Cause it looked like she wanted to do more than just carry a message for you."

"Even if that were the case, she can't do any more than I allow her to," Black said, hoping to end the discussion.

"So is that the case?"

"Not that I know of," Black lied and was glad that Bobby arrived with a female guest.

"What's up, Mike?" Bobby said and Black stood

up to allow Bobby to get to his seat. "This is—what's your name again, honey?"

"Tatiana," the woman said with attitude.

"This is Mike Black, and this is Mystique," Bobby said to Tatiana.

Black nodded at Tatiana.

"Call me Maria," she said as they passed.

"I saw CeCe on the way in," Bobby pointed out.

"Yeah, I saw her," Black said.

"You give her a message for her boy?"

"Yeah, I just talked to her," Black said and looked at Mystique. She posted a weak smile in response.

"You seen Freeze or Mylo yet?"

"No."

"They still got time to—" Bobby started to say, when he noticed Nick come into the arena, and Wanda was with him.

The decision for Nick and Wanda to come to the fight together was not one that they arrived at easily. At first, Wanda was totally against the idea, while Nick didn't see a problem with it. But after a while, Nick was able to convince her that nobody would even think twice about two friends coming to the fight together.

Not really thinking anything of it, Bobby continued. "Time to make it before the fight starts. You still haven't talked to Freeze?"

"No."

"What you gonna do?"

Black looked up and saw Nick and Wanda. "I'm gonna put this man on him," he said and stood up. "How you doin', Wanda?" He gave Wanda a hug before turning to Nick. "We need to talk. Come on."

Nick and Wanda looked at each other in horror. Freeze had told Nick what Black said about killing whoever Wanda was involved with.

Black kept walking. "You comin', Nick?"

"Right behind you," Nick said and trotted off to catch up with Black.

As Wanda watched Nick she thought about all the reasons why she was right about them not coming to the fight together. Wanda took a deep breath before turning to Bobby. "How you doin', Bobby?"

"I'm good," Bobby said and stepped aside so Wanda could get to her seat. She was about to ask Bobby what Black wanted with Nick, but that's when she noticed Mystique.

Wanda gave her a *what the fuck are you doin' here, bitch* look, and Mystique dropped her head. Naturally, Wanda had seen her at Cynt's and had heard the rumors about Black and a dancer who looked a little like Shy, but she didn't believe them. Wanda did see a slight resemblance, but no. And even if the rumors were true—and apparently they were—Wanda didn't think Black would bring her out in public.

Then Wanda looked at Tatiana. *Maybe it's take your hooker to the fight night,* Wanda thought and sat down. The fact that Bobby didn't make any comment about her coming with Nick made her feel a little more at ease, but she still wondered what Black and Nick were talking about.

"What's up, Black?" Nick asked.

Black leaned close to him and spoke slowly. "I

gotta ask you to do something, and I don't like askin' it."

"Whatever you need. You know that."

"I need you to watch Freeze."

"Freeze? Why?"

Black took a step closer and whispered. "His boy Mylo arranged for Frank to take a dive."

"What?"

"Told Frank I wanted him to do it."

"You think Freeze knew about it?"

"I don't think so, but this nigga Mylo is his boy. Keep your eye on Freeze, but you don't let Mylo outta your sight."

"I'm on them, Black," Nick said and followed Black back to their seats, relieved that Black didn't want to kill him over Wanda.

Chapter 31

When it came time for the main event of the evening, Irish Stevie Dudgeon came to the ring with a small entourage, accompanied by "*The Orange and the Green,*" an old Irish drinking song about an Irishman whose father was a Protestant and mother was a Catholic. There was a large cheering section in attendance for the fighter from Hoboken, New Jersey.

However, when it came time for Frank Sparrow to make his way to the ring, the crowd prepared for his usual big entrance, with his big entourage, lights, props, dancers, and smoke, accompanied by the live music of whatever Bronx rapper was hot at the time. But not that night.

That night, Sparrow came out with just his trainer and cut man to a recording of the LL Cool J classic, *Mama Said Knock You Out.* Sparrow always wore fancy robes and took his time getting to the ring, stopping to shake hands and greet fans, a tactic designed to make his opponent wait, but not that night. That night, Sparrow entered the arena wearing a wife beater, and he and his cornermen ran to the ring.

There was something else different about Sparrow that night. He had developed a reputation for coming out cold, therefore it always took him a few rounds to warm up; a fact Mylo counted on. That night, Sparrow entered the ring dripping with sweat.

Instead of sitting quietly and meditating about the fight as he usually did, Sparrow stood up and meditated, throwing the punches and making the feints and moves he saw in his mind. *No weaknesses,* he remembered Black telling him. Sparrow kept moving during the national anthem and the introductions, so when the bell sounded, he came out ready for battle.

When Black and Nick returned to their seats, Freeze had arrived and was sitting next to Wanda. Mylo was there as well. He was sitting on the other side of the ring in a spot where Black could both watch him and get to him quickly if it came to that. Before the fight began, Mylo was joined at ringside by Agent Masters. Bobby leaned close to Black. "Ain't that the guy from the pictures with Mylo?" he asked quietly.

"I got him."

"Yeah, but who is he?"

"A dead man," Black said as the bell rang to begin round one.

Sparrow practically ran across the ring and began working his left jab. Dudgeon, an excellent defensive fighter and a phenomenal counterpuncher, gave ground and blocked the majority of Sparrow's jabs and waited for an opportunity to get in some shots of his own.

Sparrow threw a lead right, followed by an overhand left that caught Dudgeon flush on the chin before he could counterpunch. The punch hurt Dudgeon and backed him up. Sparrow stayed with him and backed Dudgeon to the ropes with a barrage of lefts and rights. Dudgeon covered up, and finally grabbed Sparrow and held him until the referee stepped in to separate the fighters. Sparrow took two steps back, but went right back at Dudgeon when the ref resumed the action.

Dudgeon came forward, winging lefts and rights. Sparrow backpedaled, but kept working the jab. The fighters traded shots in the center of the ring. Sparrow knew from watching films of Dudgeon that he was susceptible to the lead right and the overhand left. He kept the pressure on and it wasn't long before Dudgeon once again found his back against the ropes, hurt and taking punches. Once again, Dudgeon held on and waited for the ref to come separate them, but Sparrow landed several hard rights to Dudgeon's middle section that took his breath away before the ref stepped in.

When the contest continued, Sparrow threw the lead right and practically pushed Dudgeon back. He was hurt from overhand lefts to the head and was totally defensive against the ropes, blocking some but taking hard shots from the champ, who wouldn't let up. He stepped in and threw a double-right uppercut to the jaw and followed it up with a left that dropped Dudgeon to the canvas.

The crowd, which had been on their feet since the first big punch, went wild as the referee counted Dudgeon out at two minutes and fifteen seconds of the first round.

Black could see the look of horror and confusion on Mylo's face as the ref raised the champ's hand in victory. He glanced over at Freeze; he was shouting and beating his chest like it was him who had just dropped Dudgeon. At that point, Black was sure that he hadn't betrayed him. He felt relieved that Freeze knew nothing about the fix and turned all of his attention to Mylo. Black looked at Bobby. "Tell him," he said, and kept his eyes on Mylo, who was arguing with Masters.

At Mylo's assurance that Sparrow would lose the fight by knockout in the first round, Masters had bet heavily on Dudgeon.

Bobby turned to Freeze and pulled him closer. "You know your boy Mylo tried to fix the fight."

"What? Mylo did what?" Freeze shouted over the noise.

"Had the fight fixed," Bobby said. "Set it up for Frank to take a dive in the first round until Black set him straight."

"Where that nigga at?" Freeze said, looking around the Garden.

"I got him," Black said as the ring announcer made the decision official. "Come on."

Black, Bobby, Freeze, and Nick left the ladies behind and had just begun making their way through the crowd to get to Mylo, when Sparrow jumped up on the ring ropes and pointed his glove at Mylo.

"What's he doing?" Masters said to Mylo.

Mylo looked up at Sparrow calling him out, and then turned and saw Freeze fighting his way through the crowd and coming toward him. "Shit!"

"What?" Masters shouted.

"Here comes Freeze," Mylo shouted back and he and Masters began making their way toward the aisle. Mylo looked at Sparrow on the ropes again and knew that not only had Sparrow double-crossed him, but had told Freeze about the fix as well.

This wasn't how Black wanted it to go. He wanted to be able to walk up to Mylo after the fight and take him away quietly. He hadn't counted on Sparrow getting up on the ring ropes and calling Mylo out. Now they had to fight their way through the crowd to catch up with him.

As soon as Mylo and Masters could, they quickly separated.

"Freeze. You and Nick get Mylo. Bring him to the parlor," Black said, referring to the funeral parlor that they used to dispose of dead bodies. "I'll meet you there."

"Where you goin'?" Nick asked.

"Get Mylo."

"What about him?" Nick asked quietly about Freeze.

"He's good. Just get Mylo," Black said and he and Bobby went after Masters. All they knew was that Masters was involved with Mylo in the plot to kill Black and that was enough reason to kill him.

Masters made his way out of the Garden as quickly as he could. Not knowing that Black was on to him, he wasn't in any particular hurry; he just wanted to get out of there. Masters had trusted that Mylo had the fight fixed and had bet a hundred thousand dollars on Dudgeon. There was a part of him that was glad that Freeze was after Mylo and would most certainly kill him. The operation was coming to a close and Mylo had outlived his usefulness. The plan was always to kill him. Better that Freeze kill the rogue agent than for Masters to have it on his plate.

When Masters made it to the street, he looked around for a second and began walking up Thirty-fourth Street toward Meyers Garage where he had parked his car. He gave the attendant his ticket and waited for his car, still thinking about the hundred thousand that Mylo had cost him.

As soon as the attendant was out of the car, Masters jumped in and rolled slowly toward the street. He saw, but didn't pay any attention to, the people on the sidewalk waiting for him to pull into the street. Masters didn't see Bobby nod to Black from across the street.

Black stepped up to the car with his gun drawn and fired three times. The first shot broke the glass. The next two shots hit Masters in the head. The people nearby scattered as Masters's head hit the steering wheel and the car's horn filled the air. Black put his gun away and walked away from the scene quickly.

Meanwhile, Mylo had made it out of the Garden and was trying to make it to his car. It was parked three blocks away on Thirty-fifth Street, between Fifth and Sixth Avenues. He looked back and didn't see anybody following so he slowed his pace and tried to blend in with the crowd. Mylo was startled when Freeze and Nick caught up with him in the crowd. "Where you goin' in such a hurry?" Freeze asked as soon as he was close enough to put his hands on him.

"Nowhere," Mylo said nervously. "Just tryin' to get out of here. You know, get back to the house, see how things are goin'."

"You not goin' to the after party?" Freeze asked as they walked alongside of him through the crowd.

"Yeah, I'm'a stop by there later, you know, once the real after party gets goin'."

"You oughta come ride with us," Freeze said.

Mylo knew that if he went anywhere with Freeze and Nick that they would kill him the first chance they got. There was no way he was gonna just let them take him that easy. He reached for his gun and turned to Freeze. The move caught both Nick and Freeze off guard. Mylo fired two shots to Freeze's stomach.

The crowd ran for cover at the sound of gunfire and Mylo ran away with them. Freeze grabbed his stomach, and fell into Nick's arms.

Nick gently laid Freeze on the ground. "Don't let him get away, Nick," Freeze told him as he grimaced through the pain.

Nick looked up and didn't see Mylo anywhere. He was gone. "I'm not leaving you," he said and held onto Freeze with his heart racing. "Somebody call an ambulance!" he yelled and took out his cell phone. He hit Wanda's speed dial number.

"Hey, baby," Wanda started.

"Freeze has been shot. I need you to come get this hardware before the cops get here."

"Where are you?" Wanda asked, as she picked up her pace, leaving Mystique and Tatiana behind.

"We're on Thirty-fifth Street, just before you get to Sixth Avenue. Hurry," Nick said and ended the call. Nick took off his jacket and as discreetly as he could with the crowd now closing in on them, he got Freeze's gun and wrapped it and his gun in the jacket. "Hold on, Freeze."

"You coulda gone after him, Nick," Freeze said, coughing up blood. Nick knew Freeze was right, he should have gone after Mylo, but he also knew he was right not to leave his friend.

Wanda moved through the crowd as quickly as she could in a tight dress and stilettos. She could hardly believe what Nick had just told her. Freeze had been shot. *Where the fuck am I gonna hide two guns,* Wanda wondered as she dialed Bobby's number.

He and Black had made it back inside the Garden and had just gotten to the champ's dressing room. Black wanted to be seen there in case he needed an alibi for killing Masters. "Bobby, Freeze has been shot!" Wanda shouted as soon as Bobby answered.

Bobby quickly turned to Black. "Freeze been shot."

"Give me that," Black said and snatched the cell out of Bobby's hand. "What happened, Wanda?"

"I don't know," said an out of breath Wanda. "Nick just called me and said he got shot."

"Where are they?"

"On Thirty-fifth street, just before you get to Sixth Avenue. I'm on my way there now."

"On my way," Black said and ended the call.

When Wanda got to them, the paramedics had arrived and were working on Freeze. Nick was explaining to two police officers that a man he had never seen before just walked up and shot his friend.

"Just walked up outta nowhere and shot him, huh?" asked the disbelieving officer.

Wanda pushed her way through the crowd and ran up to Nick. "Oh my God, baby, what happened?"

"Somebody just shot him and ran off," Nick said and handed Wanda his jacket. Wanda felt the weight of it and knew the guns were in there.

The paramedics had Freeze on the stretcher and Nick walked away from the officers and followed them to the ambulance. Black got there just in time to watch the ambulance drive away.

Chapter 32

Mike Black

Three Days Later

Freeze is dead.

I can't believe it. First Cassandra, now Freeze. I got to St. Vincent's Hospital in time to see Nick walking out of the emergency room. I knew just from looking at him that Freeze was gone.

Jamaica arrived in the city this morning. Me, Bobby, and Nick met him at the airport. It had been years since Bobby and Jamaica had seen each other. The last time was at my wedding. Too bad it had to be for this. After he told me how sorry he was about Freeze, he delivered a message. "Message? From who?" I asked, even though I knew.

"Jacara."

"What did she say?"

"'Er make me promise to say that you should have come see she that night before you go. But instead you run away like a scared child. But 'er say she understand. 'Er say she know she have that effect on men."

I really didn't mind what she had to say, especially since it was true. But why did Jamaica have to say it in front of Bobby?

"Oh. You left out the part about you runnin' away," Bobby said and he and Jamaica laughed all over themselves. That's why he did it, and I deserved that.

"Is that all you came here for?"

"Me come for Freeze," Jamaica said, no longer laughing.

We would lay him to rest the next day.

Wanda got a call from Kirk, which came as no surprise. Since it happened in Manhattan, it wasn't Kirk's case. But once he heard that Freeze was the person that got killed at the fight, he had to come see me. I met him at Cuisine that next afternoon. Kirk came without Richards so I knew that in addition to Freeze, he wanted to talk about DeFrancisco. After he relayed his condolences, he got to the business at hand. "So tell me what happened."

"I don't know. I wasn't there. By the time I got there he was already in the ambulance. And why do you even care, Detective? This ain't your case."

"I know it's not. I'm just askin'," Kirk said.

He started to say something else, probably to justify why I should talk to him, but I cut him off. "No, Kirk, you're a cop askin' questions. In my experience, that's never a good thing."

"Why don't you tell me anyway."

"You already know as much, if not more, than I know, or you wouldn't be sittin' here." I laughed a little. "Like you would show up here unprepared. Not happenin'."

"Okay. I know what Nick told the uniforms, and

what he will tell the detectives whenever they get around to reading Freeze's file and realize who he is."

"A fact that I'm sure you'll be glad to point out to them."

"Naa-h, I'm not trying to create any more work for myself."

"Good. 'Cause you know as well as I do that once they figure out who Freeze is, they're not gonna care who killed him and won't put too much effort into finding out unless you point them in a direction. So why don't you tell me what you know."

"That some guy just walked up and shot Freeze twice. I know nobody really saw anything except a black man running away with a gun. But you and I both know that ain't what really happened."

"What really happened, Detective?"

"I don't know. I wasn't there. I was just wondering if this had anything to do with the Commission?"

"I don't know. I wasn't there. But you know I'll find whoever did it. I promise you that. He won't be able to hide for long." I paused for effect. "Is this the part where you ask me to let the police handle it, Detective?"

Kirk laughed and so did I. That's twice I've seen him laugh. I didn't think Kirk laughed; he's always on the job. In a lot of ways, he reminds me of me. Makes me wonder what kind of cop I would have been. And then I came to my senses.

"No, nothing like that," Kirk said, still laughing. "I just wanna know if I should be expecting more bodies?"

"From what I hear, there is no more commission. They went underground screamin' peace."

"Don't want any parts of you, huh?"

"I guess not. And believe me, I been lookin'," I assured the detective.

"Yeah, I know. You and Bobby been rollin' around callin' these kids out since we talked about it. Heard you even got word to big Darryl about his brother."

"Not much gets by you, Detective. You been keepin' on top of this."

"Just trying to stay ahead of it, that's all."

"Like the good cop you are. And I mean that as a compliment."

"I took it as one," Kirk said and got ready to leave. "Oh, one more thing."

"What's that, Detective?"

"Your boy DeFrancisco escaped while he was being transferred on Friday. With the history you have with him, I just thought you should know."

"I'll keep an eye out for him," I promised, but I knew it wouldn't be necessary. I knew that old wood house in the middle of nowhere would burn to the ground and no one would find it for months, maybe years.

Kirk stood up. "Sorry about Freeze, Black. I mean that."

"Thank you, Detective," I said to Kirk and he began walking away. But then he stopped.

"The Commission is done, huh?"

"That much I can assure you, Detective."

And I could.

CeCe arranged for Stark to meet me on the upper level at ESPN Zone in Times Square. Just the two of us. I had to give CeCe credit. She got it done for me and did it quick. Maybe there was more to her than just being fine as hell. I wondered how long it would take her to put herself in some situation when she would be alone with me. There was no question about it. I was gonna end up fuckin' CeCe.

Like I said, it's kind of a rule. A woman can't set the pussy out the way she was settin' it out and a man not get it. Especially a fine-ass woman like CeCe. But for now, I was content to keep it business. She was a dangerous woman and I knew it, but that's what makes it interesting.

I met Stark at the Zone at ten o'clock that same night I met Kirk. Even though I promised to meet Stark alone, Nick insisted on coming with me. He really hasn't left me since it happened. I knew he felt responsible, especially since I told him to watch Mylo and Freeze is dead anyway. I don't blame him for that. This is a dangerous game we play and people die. It's fucked-up, but it is what it is.

Nick went in before I did wearing a disguise and was sittin' there when Stark came in. He brought two guys with him. After they scanned the room for familiar faces, they sat down and Stark came upstairs.

I finished my drink and stood up when I saw him coming toward me. "Thank you for agreeing to see me." I extended my hand in friendship and respect and he accepted it.

"I'm sorry about Freeze," Stark said.

"Yeah, so am I."

I am so tired of people beginning conversations

with me with the words, *I'm sorry about. . . .* First Cassandra and now Freeze. Who's next? Bobby? I didn't even want to think about losing my brother. "Please, have a seat." I flagged down my waitress.

"Thank you," Stark said and sat down.

"What are you drinkin'?"

"Jack Daniel's, on the rocks," he said.

"Another Remy for you?" the waitress asked.

"If you don't mind."

"Not at all," she said and walked away, swinging her hips.

"Mylo, huh?" Stark said.

"He wanted to make it look like we were at war. After y'all were dead, cops are lookin' at me while he takes over your business."

"I can see that now," Stark admitted.

"I know it was his idea for y'all to get together. Buy more product that way."

"But his real point was you. He was always pushin' that shit hard. That you were coming after us," he said as the waitress brought our drinks.

"What I wanna know is how he got with y'all?" I asked when the waitress left.

"You don't know?" Stark asked smugly.

"Know what?"

"Mylo used to buy from Birdie. I don't mean to speak ill of the dead, but he said he was doin' business right under Freeze's nose," he said like he knew he had the upper hand, and he did, 'cause I had no idea.

"Yeah, I know. He had Freeze completely fooled." I hated to admit it, but it was true. Mylo had worked his way inside my house and had done more damage than I ever thought possible.

This wouldn't have happened if I was runnin' my own show. I definitely wouldn't let that nigga run my game. If he wasn't runnin' the game, he would never have been able to get close to Frank.

What was Freeze thinkin'?

He was thinkin' that Mylo proved his value and loyalty by snitchin' on Birdie and Albert after they tried to have him and Nick killed. I understand the logic, but damn, it was fucked-up in this case.

"But I want you to know—and I mean this—you and I don't have a problem. We never have. Just as long as your business doesn't conflict with mine," I told him.

Stark sat up a little straighter in his chair like he was finally taking me seriously again. "So, just exactly what is you sayin'?"

"All I want is peace. All that shit about me killin' drug dealers for sport is bullshit. I don't give a fuck how you make your money. Your hand ain't in my pocket. So as long as you keep your hand out of my pocket, we don't have no issue." I didn't think it was really necessary to threaten to kill him if he did. I think he got the point.

"All I wanna do is make money. You make yours your way, I'll do my thing. I got nothing but respect for you, Black. Believe that."

"Then maybe you might help me with something?"

"What's that?"

"Mylo."

"What about him?"

"I need to know where to find him." I hated humbling myself like that, but he knew Mylo better than I did, so I needed him.

"CeCe said he was dead."

"He shot Freeze before he got away. You know where he might hide out?"

Stark took a sip of his drink and thought for a second. "I might know someplace. Me and Mylo was hangin' out in Philly and he took me to this house. I didn't go in with him and he wasn't in there for long, but when he came out he said every once and a while you gotta check on your foundation."

"Where in Philly?"

Stark told us where to find the house. It was in a little town outside of Philly called Marcus Hook; a three-bedrooms, three-story, single-family house on West Third Street.

The house was in darkness when me and Nick got there. I wanted to go alone. I wanted to be the one to kill Mylo, but Nick said that he had to be the one to kill him. I understood.

We sat outside for about an hour and didn't see any movement inside. We walked up on the house and Nick disabled the alarm, put on his night vision glasses, broke in the back door, and searched the house while I played sentry and waited outside. I hate waiting.

When I saw Nick come out of the house, we went back to the car.

"House is empty," Nick said. "Two-car garage, family room on the ground level. Living room, dining room, kitchen on the second level. Three bedrooms up top. I could tell somebody had been there recently. But I could tell that nobody had been there for a while before that."

"Really? How could you tell that?" I asked.

"All the food in the refrigerator was bought recently and there's dust everywhere."

"So we wait."

We had been there for a couple of hours, neither of us really saying too much. I was thinkin' about Freeze, and I just assumed that Nick was too. I was thinking about Michelle too. I had to do everything I could to keep all this violence away from her. For the time being, I felt like she was safe on the island with my mother and Jamaica watching over her, but I know anything can happen and there was nothing I could do about it.

I thought about Cassandra, and before too long, Mystique was on my mind. I really wasn't trying to get hooked up with another woman that soon after Cassandra, but there I was, claiming her, as Bobby put it. I wondered what I was doin' with her and how far I was willing to let it go.

I heard Nick take a deep breath and then he turned to me. "I got something I need to tell you, Black."

"You don't have to say it, Nick. I don't blame you; no one does."

"That's not it. I know nobody is blamin' me, but I still gotta be the one to take his life. But that ain't what I gotta tell you."

"What, then?"

"It's about Wanda."

"What about Wanda?"

"I'm the one she's been seeing," Nick said and looked away.

I wasn't ready for that one. I mean Nick could have told me anything else, but I definitely was not expectin' that. "How long this been goin' on?"

"Since you were in jail," Nick confessed.

"And y'all been keepin' it on the low for all this time?"

"Yeah."

"Wanda's idea?" It had to be.

"Yeah."

"Wanda know you doin' this?"

"No," Nick answered.

"Good. Then this stays between us. Wanda can tell me when she's ready." I thought for a second about how I felt about Wanda and Nick. "Freeze told you what I said?"

"Yeah."

"I'm not gonna kill you, Nick. I've lost too much already. If you were some other nigga, you'd be dead now," I said and laughed a little. "But I know you'll be good to Wanda. Treat her with respect."

"I promise I will."

"So, is that wedding bells I hear?" I asked when I saw headlights coming down the street and then the garage door began to open. Nick put on his night vision glasses again to try and get a look at the driver. "That him?"

"Can't tell. He's black, that's about all I could tell."

"Let's go see if it is Mr. Mylo," I said and started to get out of the car.

"Black?"

"Yeah."

"I gotta kill him," Nick said.

"It's your show," I said and got out of the car.

While we moved toward the house, the light on the second floor came on. The lights on the third floor were on by the time we reached the house. We entered the house the same way and made our way up the stairs with our guns out.

As soon as we hit the top of the stairs, the shooting started. The first thing Nick did was shoot out the lights. Two lights, two shots, which was fine for him, 'cause he had on those fuckin' glasses, but I couldn't see shit. "You all right?" Nick asked.

"Yeah."

"Stay here," he said and ran off.

Like that was gonna happen. As soon as my eyes adjusted to the dark, I moved out of the stairwell. I heard shots and moved toward them. Then I heard one of them on the steps. I found my way to the steps and went up slowly.

When I got near the top of the steps, I saw somebody in the shadows. I pointed my gun in that direction.

"It's me," Nick said just loud enough for me to hear him.

I lowered my weapon and stood next to him. With less light than there was downstairs, I tried to make out the setup. There was a room directly across from us that looked like a bathroom. There were three other doors. One room was right next to the steps, one next to the bathroom, and the other was down the hall. The only light on the third level was coming from the room at the end of the hall. Probably from a window.

"Stay close to me," Nick said.

"It's your show," I said and followed Nick toward the bathroom. He flipped on the light and checked the shower. The room next to the bathroom and the room down the hall were both empty, I mean *empty*.

No furniture, nothing. If he was still in the house, he had to be in that last room.

We moved back down the hall until we reached the door. Nick pointed to the stairwell next to the door and I moved to the side of the door. Nick steadied himself before he kicked in the door and then ducked in the bathroom as Mylo fired at the door. When the shooting stopped, I watched Nick dive into the room. I heard more shooting and ran in behind him.

I got in the dimly lit room just in time to see Mylo raise up from behind the bed ready to fire. Before I could get a shot off I saw Nick laying on the floor. He fired on Mylo. I couldn't tell how many shots he hit him with, and I didn't stop to count, but it was a lot.

When we got down to the car and away, I asked Nick, "What was that diving thing you did?"

Nick laughed a little. "Since I searched the house, I knew he could only hide in the walk-in closet or behind the bed. The angle from the closet was bad, so he had to be behind the bed. Better line of sight to the door."

"Right."

"I knew you would come in after me and that would draw him out so I could get him."

"So you used me as a decoy?"

"Basically."

"It's all good, you got him."

"Now Freeze can rest in peace," Nick said and crossed himself.

One more to go, and then Cassandra can rest in peace . . . and maybe I can find peace too.